I0517130

Miss Alice

By Sarah Gastright

Deep Sea Publishing

Copyright Page

Miss Alice-Copyright © 2014 by Sarah Gastright

ISBN-13: **978-1-939535-48-1**

ISBN-10: **1939535484**

E-Book ISBN-13: **978-1-939535-40-5**

E-Book ISBN-10: **1939535409**

www.deepseapublishing.com

Printed in the United States of America

Table of Contents

"Imagination is more important than knowledge. For knowledge is limited to all we now know and understand, while imagination embraces the entire world, and all there ever will be to know and understand."

-Albert Einstein

"Love me or hate me, both are in my favor. If you love me, I'll always be in your heart. If you hate me, I'll always be in your mind."

-William Shakespeare

Prologue

Dawn light slips through the window, bathing the room in a gentle glow. A young girl sleeps in a too-big bed with dreams in her head as peaceful and light as they could possibly be. Her door opens and a woman glides into the room. Sitting on the edge of the bed the woman places a hand on the girl's shoulder, stirring the child gently from sleep.

"Alice, it is time to awaken," the woman says gently, softly.

Groggily, Alice sits up, rubs her eyes and yawns. After a minute or two, Alice's face brightens and stares at the woman excitedly.

"Is Father home today?" Alice asks.

Nodding, the woman says, "Yes and we are both spending the day solely with you, Alice." Standing up, the woman walks to Alice's closet. "Now, what dress should you wear today?" Quickly, Alice jumps from her bed and grabs one of her favorite dresses. It is pale blue, the material light and soft, and a white sash across her stomach, tying into a bow in the back. "A very fine choice, my love! Put your hands up and let me get it on you. Hurry up now!"

Smiling, Alice puts her hands up and is quickly dressed. Her mother combs her pale hair gently but thoroughly before braiding it, a pale blue ribbon at the end of her braid to match her dress. Taking her mother's hand, Alice is walked to the Dining Room where her father sits. Although the papers on the table are obviously from work, he sets them aside to come over to his daughter. He picks up Alice with a grunt and hugs her kindly before setting her back down.

"Pull up a seat, Alice," he says. "I would love help in some of this work. Melody, are you going to prepare us a breakfast today?"

"I am," she replies with a smile. "Breakfast will be out with haste. Try not to bore her Marcus. This is our day with her to have fun."

"I do not mind helping Father," Alice says brightly. She pulls over a chair and climbs in, resting on her knees to be able to read the papers correctly.

Chuckling, Melody walks into the kitchen, shaking her head. Alice and her father make some progress in the work but Marcus has to make many changes to the paper with her assistance, no matter how earnestly she tries. She has not begun school yet so no matter how hard she tries it becomes quite taxing on Marcus with Alice's help. Marcus takes the time to teach her the basics of this land, the land she will one day inherit, but his attention is elsewhere.

Once breakfast arrives a maid takes the papers back to Marcus's study and the family happily eats their fill of Melody's wonderful spread. They joke without worry, everything very light hearted. Alice laughs until her stomach hurts and eats until she can barely move. Once the plates have been cleaned and cleared, the family moves out of the manor with Alice still giggling. Her parents each hold one of her hands as they walk towards town.

Melody's gray eyes stay bright as she watches her child play around, moving a lock of wheat colored hair from her pale face. She catches her husband's sad blue eyes and whispers a sharp warning to him. Alice looks up at her parents to see what the matter is but her father's face is instantly happy again as Alice looks up, Marcus making a joke to reaffirm the light atmosphere.

Their first stop is the bakery. Alice runs inside, her parents coming quickly behind her. They scold her lightly but the owner pushes their worries away.

"Marcus, take off your hat," Melody scolds. "It is very impolite of you to keep your hat on indoors."

"But Melody—"

"Take it off. Now."

Sighing, he takes off his hat and Alice is struck, once again, by her father's hair. Compared to many men, he is quite young but his hair is bleached silver. He usually wears a hat to cover his hair but Melody, a stickler for politeness, always makes him take it off indoors. He was hoping, on a day for happiness, that she would lay off the rules but apparently not.

The owner laughs and pats Marcus's back heartily. "Count your blessing, lad," he says. "At least you still have hair."

Marcus gives a tight smile. "Very true," he says and then presses Alice up to the counter.

"Hello Miss Princess!" the owner says jovially. "What are we here for today?"

"A big box of cream puffs!" she says, holding her arms wide. "This big of a box."

Grinning, the owner pats her head and gets her a small box. When he hands it to Alice, her eyes shining with excitement, he says, "I added a few trial puffs in there. Strawberry and apple filling in a few of them but most of them are the original kind. Let me know what you think about them, okay?"

Nodding, Alice hands the man the money that Melody gave her and the man laughs again, telling them to come back again soon.

"The King's daughter comes here often, I guess?" a customer asks the owner.

"Not so much Melody or Marcus as the little one, his only grandchild," the owner replies with a smile. "She's a good kid. I hope she keeps her attitude like that."

"No kid growing up in a royal family can stay that happy," the customer replies sorrowfully.

"Isn't that the truth?" He takes the customer's order and, when he comes back with a box to start packing, he looks back up to the customer. "But I've seen that kid outside of the bakery. In the manor, on a walk, in introductory lessons, and even when she's being fitted for a dress and she's never as happy or as excited as when she comes here to buy her silly pastries. If she ever did become cold and uptight like all the other royals, I certainly hope she could still find minimum pleasure in buying a pastry. Honestly I look forward to seeing her every month." He shakes his head with a smile. "That kid is destined to be a great Queen."

The customer snorts. "Maybe if she had a King to control her."

Handing the customer his order, the owner says, with complete seriousness, "That girl does not require a King to be a great Queen." Putting a smile back on his face, the owner lets go of the box and waves. "Do take care, sir. Come back again soon!"

As the customer leaves, he heads towards the park where he is meeting an old friend. He waits on a bench and then sees the little kid again. He sees her smiling with the mostly empty box in her hands, but he can tell that the smile she has on now is not quite the same as it was in the bakery. She runs around for a bit before nearly tripping. Her mother scolds her but the scolding goes over the child's head. She tries talking with the other kids but they hurry away from her. From afar he sees the kid walk back to her parents, who make her walk between them now.

"Oh sorry I'm late!" the customer's friend says. "Hey, isn't that the King's daughter other there?"

"Yeah, the whole family," the customer replies thoughtfully.

"What's wrong?" the friend asks.

He watches the family for a little longer before shaking his head. "Nothing. Nothing at all."

8

After a whole day out Alice is exhausted and nearly falling asleep on her feet. Her parents keep her up, holding her hands to make sure she does not trip. They refuse to carry her, not wanting her to simply expect that someone will always pick her up. They want her to learn to support herself without the help of others.

"Did you have a good day today, Alice?" Melody asks.

Alice smiles happily before nodding to them. "I wish we could spend more days like this." She yawns and almost trips over her own feet.

"Well, we will have to make room for these trips more often," Marcus replies, patting his daughter's head affectionately. She smiles happily at them.

Once they get back inside the manor they send Alice to her room. "We will wake you up for dinner," Melody tells her. "Go rest for now."

Nodding, Alice stumbles to her bedroom. Instead of going their separate ways Melody and Marcus move to their Meeting Room. Marcus sits in a chair and covers his face with his hands.

"Elbows off the table," Melody says halfheartedly. She falls into her chair and then grabs her husband's hands. "Marcus, the last day will be the best for her. That is all that matters, dear. We have prepared her the best we can and have given her the best of days."

"She is only *five*, Melody," he says. "We will be leaving her as a five year old. She is not ready to step into this world of liars and murderers." He sighs and shakes his head. "What kind of parents are we?"

"My father will take all precautions to ensure her safety and success," she replies sadly. Their large clock tolls six times. Melody squeezes her husband's hands and they stand up. A maid brings in a guest, a thin woman with red eyes.

"Your time is up," the woman says. "Our contract has been fulfilled."

Nodding, Marcus goes up to her. "We made our wish to protect our daughter," he says. "As long as she is alive and well, then I believe that you have fulfilled our contract."

"We cannot thank you enough for what you have done for us," Melody says, taking the pale girl's hands in hers. "I hope we are able to fulfill our side of the contract equally as you have."

Wings, torn and bony, erupt from her back, blocking out all remaining light. "I am sure you will."

Alice's eyes flutter open. She hears the clock toll six times and sits up. Rubbing her eyes, she looks around for what woke her up. Then she sees her door open slowly. Outside her door is a shadow the size of a grown man. She catches his smile but then he disappears behind a corner. He pokes his head out from the corner and waits. His face is shrouded to her and, even though Alice knows better than to follow strangers, she feels compelled to follow him.

"Who are you?" she whispers as she climbs from her bed. As soon as the shadow sees her moving, he disappears behind the corner and Alice quickly follows. He does not appear outside of the shadows and Alice knows it will be completely dark soon. He holds out a hand to her and, just as she is about to take it, he slips farther down the hall.

"How did you get in here?" she calls, hurrying after him. Someone wraps a hand over her mouth and she freezes. He appears again in the shadows, the hand belonging to him. He puts a finger over his mouth. She clamps her mouth shut but uneasiness fills her stomach.

They continue their chase until Alice turns a corner. The only room down the hallway is her father's study, the only place she is not allowed to go. Fear claws at her and she starts to back away but someone pushes her towards the door. Alice, after a few moments, opens the door just a crack.

A scream chokes her – it becomes stuck in her throat and her legs escape from under her. A shadow rushes through her parents, slicing their legs so they cannot walk, hitting their chest so they cannot scream and slicing their stomachs so they suffer. Alice watches, her knees hitting the cold ground and her dress soaking blood in it. The shadow tears apart their bodies, exposing bone and organs but the wounds are never immediately lethal on their own.

The first to go is her mother. Her legs are sliced open so the white bone and layers of muscle and tissue are exposed. A slice across her stomach pulses blood but the killer does not stop there. In a single swift movement her head falls off and rolls towards the door.

He moves to her father whose wound is within the stomach. Abdominal organs press against his hand as he wheezes, eyelids fluttering. Then the attacker presses a hand on his throat and slowly crushes the windpipe. He dies with eyes wide and bulging.

Alice is stuck in her spot, hand over her mouth in outright terror and disgust. He puts a finger against his lips as though telling her to be quiet before disappearing. Running to her parents, Alice slips until she is coated in red. She cannot cry, cannot speak. She holds her mother and father's hand. After a minute or two, she stands up and walks to the windows – Alice realize that the curtains were pulled closed, shading the man further from her view – and then darts around. She sees a flash of black and white leave the room right before she passes out.

By the time her eyes open it is very dark outside and Alice is in much pain. Tears roll down her cheeks and she sees a very sad man next to her.

"Oh Alice," he whispers. "I am so, so sorry."

Just then, doctors come in and check Alice for anymore glass. They say that the window shattered at close range, embedding glass inside her skin. Policemen are doing an intensive investigation on the whole ordeal but so far they have not found anything. Alice dries her tears with a bandaged, aching hand and sits through their talks with a stony face and dry eyes.

A shadow follows the platinum haired Harpy inside of their King's barrier. She is placed inside a jail cell and cannot figure out why. She is a victim here, not the culprit. Soon, the shadow comes over to her cell and looks at her with an apologetic smile.

"You better be happy for this cell right now otherwise you would be dead," the Harpy hisses, her face shifting slightly under her anger. Her wings are covering her now but she knows that attacking this man right now will not help her. "What in the world were you thinking? They were *mine*. They were contracted to *me*!"

"You complicated things with your actions," is all he says. Without another word he disappears into the shadows and she screams at him, demanding for him to get back.

By the time guards come to retrieve the Harpy her skin has freckled with small dots of red where she has been restraining her form with great effort. They yank her to a great hall where a young boy waits for her, a disapproving look on his face.

"You are the Harpy, then," he states. "You have broken a major rule, Harpy. Do you know what that rule is?"

"I am the victim here!" she screams. "You should be doing this to the man that killed them!"

"I asked you a question," he bellows. She pulls herself back, surprised by the boy. "You will answer your King and only speak when I ask the questions. If you say anything not relating to the question I have asked I will not hesitate to kill you this instant. Do you understand me?"

A shiver runs down her body, but she nods. "Yes, my King."

"Good. Now what rule have you broken, Harpy?"

Turning her head away she has to compose herself for a moment before staring at the young boy. "I was planning to take the Core of a human I did not have a legal Contract with."

"As I understand, this is your first offense. Is this correct, Harpy?"

"Yes, my King."

For a long time, there is only silence. She looks up and sees the young King, not looking older than a boy of twelve. His eyes shift colors rapidly and each time it makes her more and more uncomfortable.

"For such an offense I should restart you, Harpy," the King states. "This is your first offense ever so I feel the need to be lenient." He pauses and his eyes shift colors. She gasps when she realizes she knows the color. They lie on the color of Melody's eyes and then shift to the color of Marcus's. Finally they shift to a slightly off color of Melody's eyes, much younger and colder eyes. After a moment they race into different colors. "It seems you injured a human in the making as well. Evading capture too? My, my, what a mess you have made little Harpy. For all the scales I measure your actions on, you will be placed as a barrier watcher."

All the air escapes her as she looks at the King.

"You will be stationed at the creature gatekeeper's barrier. If you follow the rules and do well then you will regain your status in maybe four or five hundred years." He shrugs. "That is the cost of your mistake, Harpy. As I said earlier, I am feeling lenient. You should feel grateful."

She cannot move or speak. Guards take her out of the barrier and place her in front of the creature gatekeeper's barrier. She sits there until dawn comes up and with it, a shadow appears. A glob of moving shadows and the Harpy hisses, wing erupting from her back threateningly.

"Good morning to you as well."

"What do you want?" she yells. "You have destroyed my life now."

When the shadow materializes, she sees the man she had once been allied with. He was the man who mentored her upon her creation and now he has destroyed everything they built up.

"I wanted to apologize to you," he says. "Once I become King, I will free you of these binds. Please understand that what I did was truly necessary."

"Then you should be suffering this fate, not me," she snarls.

He simply smiles and then disappears into the shadows.

A few years pass and Alice hurries out of her manor, dashing past the guards and maids. She ignores their frantic calls and just runs. She weaves through people, keeping her head down as to not attract attention, before landing herself in the park. She goes to the most deserted place within the park and sits down. Taking in deep breaths, she tries her best to calm herself down but to little avail. Her teacher is quite annoying and cannot understand her frustration.

Someone comes up behind her and Alice spins around. In front of her stands a man with dark hair and red eyes. Alice takes in a sharp breath and backs away from him. He smiles warmly at her and she freezes. Many men and women have come to her with red eyes but not one has looked at her kindly.

"You must be the Princess," he says kindly, bending down to be nearly as short as Alice. "Perhaps I could be of assistance to you, Princess. I hear that you have not yet found the killer of your family."

"Get away from me," she snarls as her back hits a tree. "Whatever you are get away."

"How rude of you," he says. "If you are still ignorant let me enlighten you. I am a Demon and I am quite willing to assist you in finding your parents' murderer. You have had others come to you and request such a thing, although they probably asked more along the lines of contracting with you, did they not?"

Alice pauses and narrows her eyes at the Demon. He smiles at her before getting up to move closer before dropping to the ground to meet her at almost eye level. She watches his red eyes and they watch hers.

When she feels his hand on her chest, she slaps him as hard as she can. He spirals backwards and looks at her oddly. Crossing her arms, Alice blushes slightly. To the man she looks more angry then embarrassed. He laughs at her, holding his cheek in surprise.

"You are better than I expected," he says quietly to himself.

"Go away!" Alice snaps. "I came here to be alone and I do not want to contract with any Demon. I will find the man on my own."

"If you contract with me then the Demons will stop coming to you," he offers. "I can provide just about any service."

"I said no!" She goes to leave when he grabs her wrist. Alice spins around to slap him but he grabs her other wrist.

"Can I sell myself better? It will be a worthwhile deal if you contracted with me."

"You are a Demon and I am to be Queen. Not only is it sacrilegious to ever side with a Demon, it would soil my face in the public. Take your hands off of me this instant and leave me alone."

Letting her go, the man appears behind her, whispering in her ear, "No one will see my eyes unless they are contracted with a Demon nor will they ever notice. The public will never have to know."

"I gave you my answer and it will never change." Moving quickly, she kicks his shin and then runs out of the forest, back to her manor and peaceful gardens. No one will be able to get into her manor that is not first passed with Alice.

As soon as she reaches the wall to her garden, at the very back of her manor, she spots the man again and she bristles.

"Leave me alone."

"I will today but do not expect me to stay away forever." He opens the gate and gallantly bows. "You will be my contracted and that is all that matters. I will wait until you agree."

"You will be waiting a very long time. Good day and goodbye."

She slams the gate loudly and three guards come to get her. Once at her doorstep, she looks over her shoulder to see if the Demon is still there. To her surprise he has disappeared. She takes a deep breath of relief before steeling herself for another lesson on proper manners.

Another Demon has left the manor and the Demon King sighs in boredom. Nothing exciting ever happens in the barrier in which he is practically forced to reside in. Every day he goes through the same motions. A few misbehaving Demons are placed before him to weigh their actions. Their good deeds are less and less. He always finds it humorous how a Demon can do "good" and how the "good" actions cause such suffering. The "bad" actions are always a thin line away from "good" anyways. Often times an action is completely blurred between the lines set by previous Kings.

Between those dull times when no one is within his manor he busies himself with watching the Demons within his kingdom. If there was a prisoner here that was to be punished he would watch their lives – both their living human life and their Demonic life – and it would busy him for quite some time but there has been no one to watch in some time.

With a sigh his eyes flicker to red and he sifts through all the Demons he has punished in seconds. He pauses when he gets to the Harpy he had placed at the barrier. She is remembering a conversation between two passing men. He gladly plunges himself in the memory.

"Have you heard about the King's family?" one man asks.

The second nods sadly. "What a shame. To only have that singular bloodline must be terrifying for him. Imagine if the child died of illness."

"Let's hope that doesn't happen." They both pause for a bit before the first speaks up again. "Did you hear about how the Princess reacted? The police came to speak with her and she apparently didn't even cry! How odd."

"She's probably been traumatized from the experience. She saw her family murdered, after all. That probably caused irreparable damage to the child's mind."

"True but...."

"But what?"

"I mean, if she's to be the next ruler then I worry about that kind of coldness, you know? No empathy can be just as bad as too much."

"It'll pass over, I'm sure. After all she is a royal. The doctors in her manor are probably fixing her up as we speak."

"Very true!"

Snapping out of the memory, the Demon King wonders about the little human he had only briefly seen a very short time ago. She had cried, and the Demon King had seen it! Perhaps only a tear or two but it was still crying, was it not? Regardless, his curiosity wins out over him. He takes in a breath and closes his eyes. When he opens them again he sees the little human running towards the forest. How boring.

He brings himself back and shrugs, not seeing what makes her so curious. His mind wanders to the people within her kingdom and then his guards bring him Demons to judge. He renders his judgment and slumps against his throne again. What a bore, living as a ruler. He thought it would be much more fun when he beat the previous King.

After some thinking he grows curious again of the human. Someone had slaughtered her family to prevent a Demon from taking their Cores. From what he had seen through the injured human's eyes she had been led to the crime by someone. What was so special about the human family? What is so special about the girl? The Demon King knows that it could not have been a human who killed her family, as the Harpy would have easily taken care of things. So what drove a Demon to do this?

With spiked curiosity he settles into his throne and lets his eyes flash to gray.

Chapter 1

A plate whistles through the air, hitting the wall and screeching as it shatters.

A petite girl turns to an older man, her eyes flaming in rage. "How dare you try to poison me with that filth?" she demands, spitting the words with venom. "I have half the mind to fire you now!"

"Miss Alice," says the man, unaffected by the girl's rage. He is amused by her anger; feeds from her temper but he bows his head to hide his disrespect. "Forgive me for my error."

Crossing her arms, the girl brings up her chin and stares at him indignantly. "That would be *Princess* Alice to you, Anthony," she snaps, but then she calms herself slightly. "Anthony, what did I ask for?"

Anthony lifts his head in surprise. "A pomegranate torte with a single scoop of vanilla ice cream on the top, Miss Alice," he says.

"And what did you bring me?"

Glancing at the wall, Anthony sees the smeared cake falling in clumps to the ground. "A lemon cake with a poppy seed and honey glaze, Miss Alice."

"How can you possibly get lemon and pomegranate mixed up?"

For a moment Anthony considers not answering but he knows, from past experience, that her true anger is much more threatening. Attractive yes, but nonetheless ferocious and terrifying. For Anthony, a powerful Demon, to ever consider using the word "ferocious" to describe a mere human is a rare event. So Alice's anger is something quite unique. Then again, that is one reason why Anthony picked her.

"Perhaps it was kitchen mix up," Anthony says. "I was not the one to make your meal today, Miss Alice. I was preparing your Show Room for Mister Edgar Runwell."

"Do I have a meeting with the Runwells today, Anthony?" Alice asks in confusion. "I thought that was a few more days away."

"Miss Alice, you baffle me with your absent mindedness," Anthony says with a smile. "You have a meeting to discuss the landmass in the west. He wishes to purchase that land for a considerably lower price than normal and believes that you and his son, Rowan Runwell, should marry."

Snorting, Alice slumps back in her chair and crosses her arms in anger.

A decade has passed since the fateful incident with Alice's family. Since then she has been more than a little eager to meet the man who could perform such an act on defenseless people, but has made little advancements in the case. Once she meets that man she hopes to discover his motives for it. Was it a random act or a vengeful act? Once she knows she will prosecute or forgive the man. From previous meetings Alice knows that Lord Edgar is not the killer so meeting with him has become little more than a bothersome task.

Princess Alice is a petite girl with a temper that does not match her form. At fifteen she is smaller than normal and her eyes are a bright gray that flash as sharply as a whip when she is mad. Her hair is straight and pale blonde, bleached from days in the sun and reaches her waist and her skin is pale and predominantly flawless. Her temper often gets the better of her, especially when dealing with people less knowledgeable than she. Alice expects much from the people she meets, holding them to the standards she is placed at, and is not one to back down from anything thrown at her.

Despite her petite form and lack of true physical and political power, she holds herself and others to a high set of morals. She keeps to what she feels is right, even if others see it as flawed. Many people have frowned upon her reasoning for finding the murderer of her family, but she sees it as fair. Should he have a true reason for it, would it not be easier for everyone to finally recuperate from their deaths than if it was simply a random act? Perhaps not for others, but for Alice it will put her mind at ease.

Before contracting with Anthony, Alice had been putting up with Demons appearing and wanting a contract with her for many years, all of which she refused. If not for the events that led to her contract with Anthony, she would not have a Demon by her side now.

Once they had contracted successfully Anthony informed her that it was quite rare for a human to be able to summon a Demon (let alone plural) with simply hate. Most would have to perform a kind of ritual to even speak with a Demon. Even with five or six people it takes a lot of energy from those partaking in the ritual.

In comparison to Alice's bright and small form, Anthony is quite tall and appears in his twenties with pale skin. He has dark hair that touches his shoulders, and he wears an amused smile all the time while his eyes are red as rubies and glow like fire. After many failed attempts, he happily gained the upper hand in her situation and successfully managed to convince her to contract with him.

Despite their many differences the pair do share a common thrive for power. Alice desires the control of her kingdom, to have it redrawn in her vision. Anthony longs to become the King of Demons in order to prevent some Demons from leaving, and to revisit some debts he has left undone. Both of them desire power, but their methods are quite different.

Their contract was made for Alice's desire to meet her parent's murderer and discover his reasons. After completion of both feats Anthony is to retrieve Alice's Core, which will bring him to just enough power to defeat the current Demon King and take his place as ruler. Alice is aware of the consequences of her contract – that she will never fully live once Anthony retrieves his payment. But once justice for her parent's murder is complete, what more does she have to live do?

"Will Lord Edgar reschedule?" Alice asks with a tired sigh.

"My dear Alice, you should know better than to disrespect a Lord," Anthony tells her. "Now, come along. We need to dress you before they arrive."

Groaning, Alice lets herself be dragged to her room. Anthony does not hesitate or even blink when Alice slips off her dress. She stands, her pale body shown to the whole world if they dared look, and she holds out her hand.

"My dress, Anthony," she orders.

Anthony cannot help but admire Alice. Her actions have always spoken louder than her shrillest yell, and her kindness is softer in measure than that of her angriest slap. She cannot hide the scars over her body, and she certainly does not try to hide them. Anthony cannot help his attraction to the human girl, the gravity she has, but he thinks nothing of it. He places those thoughts far away because, after all, he came to her for power. He will use Alice to her fullest potential. His curiosity of the strange human will always be second in his mind.

Rummaging through her dresser, he finds a sapphire blue dress that not only makes Alice look like a doll made from porcelain but it will hug her beautifully. Its material is silk and the skirt underneath it is white and thin. It reaches to the top of her knees, exposing her pale legs and covers her arms, letting her long fingers show. Her chest is covered but hugged and her hair glows in comparison.

"That dress for a simple Lord?" Alice says with a snort. "Perhaps you truly wish me to wed, Anthony."

"Never, Miss Alice," Anthony replies, walking over to Alice. She lifts her arms and he slips the dress over her head with a gently swish as the material cascades over her body. "You can only belong to me, Miss Alice."

"I belong to no man," she hisses, straightening her dress. "For the last time, Anthony, call me by my true title. *Princess* Alice."

Smiling, Anthony bows at the waist. "Of course, *Miss* Alice."

Sighing, Alice looks at her feet and then at Anthony. "My shoes."

"Perhaps shoeless will be more appropriate," Anthony suggests against his better judgment. "You wish to appear weak to fool them, correct?" Anthony's eyes eat up Alice's body and his amused smile never faltering.

"Yes but the floors are cold," Alice argues. "If I should catch a cold, then nothing will get done."

"Socks, then, Miss Alice," Anthony suggests.

"My black shoes, Anthony."

Giving a single laugh, Anthony walks to her closet and finds a pair of knee-high white socks and the shoes she desires. Alice is already sitting on her bed waiting when Anthony reappears.   She wishes she could hit him; she wants to hit him and it *hurt* him. Alice is not bothered by the way Anthony strokes her legs, letting his hands linger on her exposed calf longer than required. Nor does she let the way he watches her be a bother. What irritates her is that she cannot physically hurt him. She has tried for years to find his weak spot but to no avail. If she could hurt him some of her problems would be resolved.

After a little bit, Alice decides that the shoes clash too much and orders Anthony to take them off. His grin seems to grow bigger and he neatly places the shoes back in her closet. A ring at the door echoes down to her room and Alice frowns deeply.

Anthony rushes her to the Show Room, leaving her to get situated, and then he returns with two men: one only slightly older than Alice and the other much older.

Standing up, Alice curtsies politely and puts on a nice smile. "Lord Edgar Runwell, Sir Rowan Runwell," Alice says kindly. "It is a pleasure to have you in my home."

Lord Edgar takes her hand first and kisses it and Rowan follows from example.

Sir Rowan is a kind fellow. He has a childish look to his face and his brown hair is tousled today. His skin is toned from days in the sun and he is fit. Today he is in a suit like his father. Rowan's eyes are brown and warm and he has always held an affection for Alice and he has voiced it more than once to her. Alice, however, does not care for him.

Lord Edgar has gray hair with only a streak of black left and cold brown eyes. His skin is weathered, but not disgustingly so. He still seems to be of good health given his age. He appears somewhat muscular, but Alice guesses he probably had not lifted more than a stack of paper in the past year.

Lord Edgar only cares to eliminate the Millersky family, as they are the royal family and they hold the power he desires. Should Lord Edgar successfully get Rowan and Alice to marry, he would probably have Alice "disappear" and have his son inherit the power.

Alice is oblivious to Lord Edgar's true motives in his proposal to have Rowan and herself married, Anthony sees it bright and clear. He refuses to let his Alice be with someone who would simply kill her off before her part of the contract is fulfilled. Once Anthony can have Alice's Core, the humans can do with her as they please. After all, she will not be his problem anymore.

"Please sit," Alice says, sitting in her seat. "Anthony, can you please fetch something to drink? Cocoa would be good for a day like this, would you not agree?"

Lord Edgar nods. "A wonderful choice, Princess."

"I will have it right out," Anthony says, leaving them to their own discussion.

"Shall we get down to business?" Alice says as soon as Anthony is out of earshot. "You wish to buy the westward land from me, correct?"

Lord Edgar nods. "Yes and for a reasonable price. You would be ridding yourself of the poorer section of your land and you would only have to see the fancy nobles like yourself."

After a moment of consideration Alice smiles at him. "You are a smart man, Lord Edgar," she says kindly, "but you are not thinking on this correctly. Should I sell you this land with my people as well, who will feed the rest of my people? How will great crafts and rich food be brought to everyone? Yes, knowing of the poor in my land does anger me but I know better than to poke a sleeping bear."

Anthony comes back into the room and sets cocoa in front of everyone. Alice takes a sip first followed by Lord Edgar and Sir Rowan.

"For one hundred thousand, would you reconsider?" Lord Edgar asks.

Alice sets her cup on the table gently. "Perhaps you have misunderstood my words, Lord Edgar. I have no intentions of selling you the westward land. They control everything that sustains life and beauty." She closes her eyes to take a savory sip. "Maybe you would understand what life they can give, what beauty they can produce, if given the right options and tools, Lord Edgar."

For a minute or two no one speaks. Lord Edgar breaks the silence by clearing his throat loudly and saying, "Then perhaps you have considered my proposal to have you and Rowan married?"

"Lord Edgar I grow tired of your games," Alice proclaims. "You wish for more than I am willing to give. I am declining that offer as well."

"We could improve your wealth, Princess Alice," Lord Edgar argues. "You would be a fool to decline my offer."

"I would be the fool, you say?" Putting down her cup, she sends a sharp look at Lord Edgar. "Perhaps you should explain to me, Lord Edgar, what is so foolish about declining this offer. Be wary, though, as you are speaking to the head of the Millersky family and the King's granddaughter."

"Our King would certainly be happy to have his wealth improved!" Lord Edgar stands up and sends a glare at Alice. "Our King would happily sell off his poor and weak if it improved his wealth and strength. Only a fool would remain weak."

"A fool would not think things through."

"If you think you can sway me, Princess Alice, then you have yet to truly grow up. This is an adult's world, Princess Alice, and one you are sorely unprepared to step in."

Sighing, Alice slowly stands and looks at him. "Perhaps you should think wisely about your words, Lord Edgar."

"What can a single girl do against two men?"

Alice waves her hand and Anthony appears by her side in less than a blink.

"A single girl holds more than enough power to tear down everything about you, Lord Edgar," Alice comments lightly. "A single girl can block your income and burn your crops. Lord Edgar, a single girl can *ruin* you. Choose your words wisely." Alice spies him moving towards his waist where no doubt a weapon will lay. "Choose your actions even more wisely."

Lord Edgar pulls out a gun and cocks it before pointing it at Alice who simply sighs.

"Marry my son and accept my offer," he orders, "or you and your butler will perish."

"Father, you are going too far," Rowan says, slamming his hands on the table as he stands. "You must take into consideration what the King could do to you if she was found dead. She is his final heir, Father."

"She is a fool and unable to truly understand this world, Rowan," Lord Edgar replies. "What you are saying means nothing. The King cannot do anything to hurt me."

With that, Alice takes a step back. "Forgive me for my rudeness, Sir Rowan," Alice says with a smile. "Shall we take a walk? Anthony, you and Lord Edgar can finish our meeting."

"You are not going anywhere," Lord Edgar yells. Three loud shrieks breaks the silence of the room and the moment tries to regain speed and reason but to little avail.

In front of Alice's face are three bullets held in suspension by Anthony's fingers.

"You are quite slower than before, Anthony," Alice comments with disappointment. "Or are you trying to get me killed?"

Anthony chuckles. "You should know me well enough by now, Miss Alice," he says. "You will not be dying before I get your Core."

Alice laughs coldly. "Of course, how could I forget?" Her gaze falls on Lord Edgar, who looks more than a little confused. "I warned you, Lord Edgar, to choose your words and actions carefully." With that, she turns her head to the side to see Rowan. "Our walk, Sir Rowan?"

"What are you going to do to Father?" he asks.

"Who knows?" Alice replies. "I like to leave things in an air of suspense. Will he live…or die slowly?" Holding out her hand, offering it to Rowan, Alice sees him hesitate. "If you stay you will most certainly share in whatever fate he travels on."

Rowan hesitates before moving to stand by his father. "I will not betray him," he says, his voice wavering slightly. "Kill us, if you want."

"What a waste," Alice sighs. "Anthony, you can do as you wish."

"Yes, Miss Alice," he says, sending her a playful look before moving away.

Alice walks to her chair in the corner of the room right next to the curtains where sunlight shines through the windows giving shy warmth to Alice's skin. Alice watches with a cruel satisfaction as the two men are beaten and bloodied in their own game. The Lord did not learn from the first three bullets. Trying to send three more, Anthony ricochets them back, wounding the Lord and his son to the point of no chance of escape. As Alice watches the scene unfolding, she cannot help but think of a cat and mouse: the cat only stops playing when the mouse is dead. Their respectable blood taints the white carpet in a distasteful way and Alice cannot help but complain.

"Anthony, could you take these bleeding sacks outside before you soil my floors any further?" she asks, irritated that he would not think of such a matter.

"So sorry, Miss Alice," Anthony says, that grin on his face seeming to grow. *His smile mirrors that of storybook cat*, Alice thinks with a laugh. "I will clean up this mess myself."

Sir Rowan's face has lost all blood, leaving only a pale shell. He stares at Anthony, who holds Edgar's limp and mangled body in his hands. Sir Rowan takes out his own gun and shoots at Anthony, wasting bullets and providing a weapon. When Anthony sends the bullets back to Rowan, the boy's fate is thoroughly sealed. *Silly, stupid boy,* thinks Alice.

Anthony brings up his hand, his fingers appearing like claws, and reaches into Sir Rowan's chest. With a gasp of pain, Sir Rowan falls to the ground and Anthony brings up a still beating heart. A plate on the table holds the heart, and Anthony turns back to Lord Edgar. His chest rises every now and again but he is on the brink of death.

"Put them out of my sight," Alice says dismissively. "He may just live and he will forever know who not to mess with."

Alice gets off her chair and walks over to Sir Rowan's lifeless face. *What a waste*, she thinks. A nice boy really. Stupid, but nice. Not many men could be considered nice nowadays but, then again, there is little reason to be nice. After a moment Alice draws the family seal on Rowan's forehead in his own blood and then Anthony takes the Lord and his son out of the house.

Alice's cook brings in her meal which she eats with dissatisfaction, finishing her lukewarm cocoa in the process, before ordering a maid to come in and clean the mess made. She tells the maid that Anthony will be cleaning most of it later on but cleaning it to some degree now will lessen the pain of it later.

"Another bad meeting, Princess?" asks the maid. She looks at the blood on the floor and pales a bit. "I hope none of this blood belongs to you, Princess, or Mister Anthony."

"Sadly another resource wasted," Alice replies with a sigh. "No injury to us. Anthony simply had a messy fight."

Although the maid is curious about what goes on in the meetings, she keeps her questions back. From the messes made the maid does not believe she could stay alert to hear the tale. With a strong will and imagination, the maid goes to work scrubbing the carpet and floor.

"I apologize that this meeting went out of hand," Anthony says when he appears again. Alice dismisses the maid who bolts from the room. Anthony chuckles at the maid's quick departure. "I take full blame, Miss Alice."

"No worries," Alice replies. "You needed to play after everything. Can you please use my formal title, Anthony?"

Anthony grins mischievously and devours the heart whole, making Alice scrunch her nose up in disgust. After all, Alice did tell him to do with the foolish pair as he pleased. Afterwards, he slips off the red-stained gloves and finishes the cleaning left from the maid.

Alice sits in her chair, drinking another cup of cocoa and eating fruit tarts thinking of the scene that had just occurred in her Show Room. It will only take a few days for the Show Room to be presentable again. In that time, many more meetings will be arranged under her nose. Anthony will try his best to get the ones who think themselves better than the King and it will always end like this. Anyone who threatens Alice's existence must suffer greater agony than death, after all.

By night fall, as Anthony is putting Alice to bed, he cannot help but wonder what she dreams about. Does she dream of her family's murder or of the murders she ordered? Does she dream in full color, or are they monochrome with no flavor? Alice's mind is certainly not straightforward, nor is it complex. Anthony is determined to fully understand her, but he wishes not to get anymore attached to her.

"Anthony?" Alice whispers in the night. "I apologize for the events from today's meeting."

Anthony smiles at her. "You have little to apologize for, Miss Alice."

She gives a small smile. "Will you *please* use my formal name?"

"Of course, Miss Alice."

Chapter 2

"Good morning, Miss—" Anthony pauses as a pillow flies out towards his face. A dull thud greets Alice's ears but she is unaware if she actually hit him. By his small laugh, Alice doubts that the pillow reached its intended destination. "—Alice. You will be behind in your schedule if you do not wake up now."

"It is not even dawn yet," Alice grumbles, pulling up the covers a bit more. "Come back when it is dawn."

Giving a single laugh, Anthony walks over to the windows and yanks back the curtains. When he reaches the third window Alice grumbles angrily but sits up, rubbing her eyes before sending him a glare.

"Miss Alice if you keep wearing such a face it will surely freeze like that," Anthony tells her. "You would not want that, would you? Now, out of bed."

Alice slides out of her bed, hissing as the cold floor hits her feet but allows Anthony to dress her properly in a white sundress and sandals. Carefully, she combs her hair while half listening to Anthony talk about her plans for the day.

"You have lessons with Lady Belle after breakfast until mid-afternoon, lessons with Sir Smith from then to nightfall. After that you have a few errands to run in town that are still pending in importance and amount."

"Is that all?" Alice grumbles, yanking a knot from her hair. "Why do I have two lessons in one day? Is something special coming up?"

Anthony's smile twitches with humor and he cannot help but wonder what goes on in Alice's head. He knows that Alice hates lessons with Lady Belle, as Alice is anything but interested in her studies to become a "Lady worthy of a Lord," as Lady Belle would say, but she has not had a single lesson in days. Even if Alice fights her whole way through her lessons with Lady Belle, Anthony has seen the small changes in demeanor. Not that Alice would ever admit to accepting Lady Belle's teachings though.

"Nothing special is planned for this week or next, Miss Alice," Anthony tells her, "but with all your meetings, you have missed quite a few lessons."

"Can we not reschedule Lady Belle's lessons for another day?" Alice complains, putting her comb down. "It is not like I will need to know how to sew or cook. No Lord will be wedded to me."

"Perhaps one day, your mind will change, Miss Alice," Anthony replies. "Now, breakfast is served in the dining room, where Lady Belle will be discussing your new lessons while you eat."

Sighing, Alice stands up and looks at herself one last time in the mirror. Deciding she appears acceptable she lets Anthony lead her to the dining room where Lady Belle sits with her back straight awaiting Alice.

"Hello, Alice," Lady Belle says, standing up and giving a curtsy to both Anthony and Alice. "You have certainly prepared a fine meal for your guest today, Anthony."

"It is a pleasure to serve, Lady Belle," Anthony replies. "I hope you and Alice make progress in your lessons." With that, Anthony gives a short bow at the waist and leaves.

Alice, of course, is not happy. Lady Belle is a kind woman, one you expect to see caring for young children at a school or of her own. Not too surprising, she is also quick to scold but her praises mean much. Almost like a game Alice dances around Lady Belle's nerves, sometimes grating them while other times mending them.

"Today, Alice, you will be practicing table etiquette and you will be introduced to an instrument of your choice," Lady Belle begins just as breakfast is brought out.

"Why an instrument?" Alice asks before steadily eating her breakfast. Despite being starved, she would rather not hear Lady Belle's rant about her eating style being "extremely improper for a young lady like herself" for hours upon hours again.

"Every good Lord wants a Lady who can perform for him," Lady Belle replies. "I have heard from Anthony that you used to play the violin?"

Alice heaves a great sigh before plopping her elbows on the table and resting her chin on the back of her folded hands. *Traitor*, she thinks towards the door, knowing that Anthony is close by.

"Yes, a long time ago," Alice confides. "I have long since retired from playing." Alice's mother had wanted Alice to learn how to play an instrument so Alice was taught the scales and basics of the violin at a young age. After her family's death Alice plunged head first into her studies, hoping to avoid the pitying glances she received from everyone else. As she aged, her skills in academics soared but not nearly as much as her musical talent. That is how Alice dealt with the loss of everyone, all the pitying glances, the way they treated her like she would break: she would drown them out in music. Before she met Anthony, she had been playing in the park, hidden from the world, where a Demon appeared and smashed her violin to pieces when she declined his offer to contract with him. She could have gotten a new one easily, missing perhaps a day or two of practice, but Alice decided she would simply stop, telling herself that playing was childish. She has played twice before with Anthony in her company and at balls and certain ceremonies, but only ever a song or two.

"Anthony said that you are very good," Lady Belle says, glaring at Alice's elbows. "It would be a waste to throw away talent."

"I am not playing an instrument of any kind," Alice tells her with an edge to her voice. "I will sit through this whole day learning proper table etiquette and proper pronunciation of every word in the English dictionary before I pick up or even look at an instrument again."

"You will do as your instructor says," Lady Belle tells Alice, her voice suggesting that arguing is futile. "His Majesty the King wishes you to have the best education possible before you are wedded."

"You are not my mother nor is he. Neither of you have any control over what I will or will not do," Alice fires, sending a vicious glare. "The King may want me to have a proper education for when I become the wife to some Lord or Prince, but it will not change who I am and neither will a stupid instrument."

Lady Belle's eyes turn to narrow slits and she stands up. "You have no right to talk to me this way. Your behavior is out of line and extremely improper."

Alice stands up as well. "*You* have no right to talk as though you are superior to me in my manor."

"Respect for your elders surpasses the pride of your house status."

"Family status surpasses respect for elders."

Lady Belle and Alice glare at each other, neither wanting to back down. Lady Belle may only be a class below Alice but Alice will pull her superiority over Lady Belle whenever something does not go her way.

"You are acting like a spoiled child, Alice," Lady Belle finally says with an eerie calmness to her voice. Instantly Alice knows she has over stepped some boundary. "I am tired of you pulling social superiority over my head Alice and I am well aware you only do it when you have been backed into a corner you do not know how to leave. Do you think that I cannot read, Alice? I am well aware of your family situation and I was certain your behavior would blow over after time but it has only grown in intensity. I pity you Alice, but that does not mean I am willing to teach someone who refuses to listen. " With that Lady Belle collects her things and walks to the door. Anthony appears to walk Lady Belle to the door and is quite confused.

"Lady Belle, you are leaving already?" he asks.

"I believe Alice needs time to consider her priorities and to cool her head," Lady Belle replies icily. She looks back over her shoulder to say, with a raised voice, "Send me a message when you decide to be cooperative, Alice."

Anthony escorts her out and returns to find Alice looking at the ground with wide eyes.

"I have never seen Lady Belle so mad," Anthony comments. "Are you well, Miss Alice?"

Alice does not reply so Anthony walks over, more than a little curious. Is she sad? Mad? Embarrassed? Anthony is unsure so he stays cautious when approaching her. Then he hears her mumbling. Crouching down to hear her and to give some sense of comfort to Alice, he is quite unprepared for her reaction.

"She *pities* me," Alice hisses, looking at her legs as she tries to figure out why anyone would even bother with the words ten years later.

"Miss Alice, anyone would pity a child who has lost their family," Anthony states. He puts his hands on her elbows, about to beckon her up and take her to the private garden, her favorite place of the whole manor.

Alice is not quite keen on the idea. Her hand lashes out, sharp as a whip, and slaps Anthony across the face.

"I will go to the garden on my own," she snarls, pushing his hands away and storms out the room.

Anthony is stunned, unable to move from his position as he watches her leave. Only on rare occasions can Alice catch Anthony so off guard, usually in times when he cannot tell exactly what is going on in her head. Anthony knows how much Alice hates pity and what her opinion on death is. She believes, with her whole heart, that those who die should be mourned only briefly and then celebrated. Celebrate the good, the bad, the funny, the bland, the happy, the sad, but don't mourn them long. Then you should value those you have left and cherish the time. Learn and grow stronger from the loss of someone you love. Alice believes, without a doubt, that the pitying glances people give her is a sign that they have not truly moved on after her family's massacre but Anthony sees it differently. He knows that they cast her pitying glances because they know that she has not truly moved forward from the massacre. Alice may put on a strong face but those scars will never heal.

Anthony gives a sly smile as he passes a mirror. He had been coming to see if everything was okay as he had heard angry voices and was surprised to find a leaving Lady Belle. She claimed that Alice was behaving childish but she does not understand the half of it.

About a month ago Lady Belle had asked Anthony if Alice had ever played an instrument and he had not thought of her reasons when he said, "At one point, she played the violin and was quite good. She has not played in a few years though." If Anthony had been informed of her decision to teach Alice more about music, he would have intervened. Although he does not know the full reason for her dislike of the instrument now but can certainly guess the reason is attached to her family.

Late morning rays hit Anthony's face when he steps into the yard. He takes in a deep breath, and his eyes spot Alice immediately. When Alice was younger her father made a swing connected to the old apple tree, where Alice used to swing every day. She has always been fond of that very spot within her garden and she visits whenever she is mad or upset.

Her back is turned away from Anthony and her head is tilted up. He can see her gray eyes looking mesmerized by whatever she sees. Despite her happy look, he can still see her taut body, ready to spring and lash out if startled and even from the door he can see her hands gripping the rope of the swing hard enough to turn her knuckles bloodless. Anthony cannot help but smile at her, even though she cannot see him.

"Lost in a fractured paradise, Miss Alice?" Anthony asks, a grin on his face. "How fitting for you."

With a gentle swish he retreats back inside.

Alice turns her head towards the door and cocks her head to the side. "Anthony?" she asks quietly. When a bird chirps her head darts back towards the tree and she smiles again. A birds nest with four featherless chicks all poke their heads up, their beaks wide open and waiting for their parents to feed them. A female finch appears, regurgitating her meal for her babies. Smiling, Alice leans back and rocks gently in her swing.

Somewhere far in the distance thunder rolls and Anthony, standing in the manor, frowns deeply.

"Sounds like a storm's coming," says a gardener as Anthony passes by. "Mister Anthony, is all well with Princess Alice?"

Anthony offers the gardener a reassuring smile. "Everything will be fine," he replies, staring at the clouds intently. "Perhaps you should cover the gardens. I think the storm will be quite harsh."

"Yes sir, Mister Anthony!" the gardener says before hurrying off.

For a second Anthony thinks that he is imagining things. After all he is under pressure to keep Alice well and keep her from harm that always seems to find her. Then, as thunder rumbles again, Anthony knows he is not daydreaming. Just under the thunder a sound that is barely covered, but to a Demon's ears it sounds like a quiet, eerie shriek. Metal screeching paired with nails on a chalk board but at a much higher pitch. Any Demon would know the sound and they would know to fear it.

"A terrible storm indeed," Anthony mutters, his smile completely gone before turning away from the clouds and retreating into his sitting room.

Chapter 3

"Miss Alice I would recommend staying in tonight," Anthony says sternly. "It will be a harsh storm and I do not want you getting caught in it."

Alice crosses her arms and fixes him with her most stubborn look. "We have errands to run and my lessons are over for the day. You even said that they were of some importance."

Since Alice's blowup with Lady Belle, evening has fallen and the sky is darkening with every passing second. Alice's second instructor – Sir Robert Smith – came and stayed for a handful of hours before leaving in order to out run the storm that continued to build over the hours. Sir Smith is the tactician for the King's army and is in charge of preparing Alice for her future as the kingdom's ruler by teaching her as much as he can about the military's strength, the kingdom's allies, enemies, and neutral companions, while also keeping her updated on the territory's economics and well-being. In Sir Smith's opinion, Alice will make a fine ruler but he worries that her intelligence and opinion will be forgotten once a King is named with her. Sir Smith is actually against her marrying at all, but it lies on the King's shoulders to choose that fate.

"Yes but there is a storm quickly approaching," Anthony insists. "It will ruin your clothes and make it extremely dangerous for the horses as well as anyone inside the carriage."

"Never once have you been worried for my clothing nor have I ever fretted about the horses," Alice responds. "We can walk to the town, after all. It is not a long walk."

"Miss Alice that is worse than riding in the carriage."

Alice narrows her eyes at Anthony. Never once has he taken into consideration anything other than Alice's life let alone her clothes or horses. She could easily wear her raincoat or perhaps a cloak. Anthony's insistence that she stay home only makes Alice more determined to go out.

"The storm will not be here for another hour or so," Alice says. "In that time we should be able to get to town, complete our errands and get back to the manor."

Anthony's senses are strained to their possible extent. Each rumble of thunder cannot hide the sound of screeching now that he has picked it up. Each gust of wind cannot block the scent of burnt flesh, of human blood. Each shifting shadow causes Anthony tenses, preparing to block Alice from whatever may hide inside. Demons may not fear much but any Demon with half a brain knows to fear the screeches that ride thunder. Anthony would never inform Alice of the situation unless he truly needed to which is why they have been arguing since Sir Smith left. If Anthony took Alice to town, he would have no way to fully protect her and that is not something he is willing to let happen.

"Miss Alice I try my hardest not to let you get hurt," he says. "Please do not make my job any harder than it already is."

"Anthony, you have put me in danger before," Alice reminds him. "I can take care of myself just fine." Alice hears the thunder, the brief gust of harsh wind and her stubbornness falters slightly.

Anthony, seeing her resolve falter, jumps on the opportunity. "The storm is only going to get worse, Miss Alice. I know you can take care of yourself as fine as anyone but nature pities no man. All the errands can wait until the morning or after the storm passes."

A crack echoes through the empty hallway and the bright lightning illuminates the hallway. To Alice the lightning came only slightly before the thunder but Anthony could tell with much regret that the thunder came earlier. Alice shivers but is unsure why. There is a chill in the air and Alice does have a sweater on but she certainly does not feel cold. Storms have never frightened Alice. *Perhaps Anthony's worry is coming onto me*, Alice thinks.

"What are the errands we have to do?" Alice asks.

"A dress fitting for a ball, your broach pick up, and looking for more help," Anthony says. "The latter is a personal errand to run."

Blinking, Alice asks, "Why do we need more help? You have found more than enough help and have some to spare."

Anthony has always kept the manor filled with help of many kinds: maids, gardeners, cooks, musicians (for when Alice holds balls, he claims), and at least two or three doctors. All of which work and are directed by Anthony and Alice does not understand why he needs so many people. Anthony will not tell her but it does not prevent Alice from asking.

"You can never have too much help, Miss Alice," Anthony responds in his usual way when she questions him. Another thunder clap and Anthony quickly darts his eyes around, the screeching sounding closer than before. He adds a mumbled, "Especially with this storm."

Alice does not catch the last part but looks behind her shoulder where Anthony is staring. "Is something the matter Anthony?"

A flash of lightening causes Anthony to visibly jerk and Alice narrows her eyes into cold, considering slits.

"Why are you so jumpy?" she demands. "Is that why you will not let me go out? Afraid of a little storm, Anthony?"

Anthony smiles tightly, barely masking his worry. He does not smell the scent of burning flesh or blood as strongly however the screech seems to be closer.

"Perhaps we should go into town, or at least a walk around outside," Anthony says. "Come along Miss Alice. Fresh air will keep you well."

"But I thought you said—"

"Miss Alice, I ask you to trust me." He looks back at Alice, his red eyes dangerous and showing his frets more than he would ever like. "So Miss Alice do I have your trust?"

Alice does not even hesitate. "If I cannot trust you, then I cannot trust myself." Alice reaches out her hand and Anthony, with a cold smile, takes her hand and pulls her close, picking her up and rushing as fast as he can out of the manor. A strong gust of wind hits them and Anthony tucks Alice's head carefully to his chest. He can feel her cheeks heat up and he hears Alice murmur something but does not hear it over the wind and sudden thunder.

The stench of human blood permeates the area around the manor and, as the thunder booms, the screeches become painful. Looking around Anthony tries to find out where the sounds are coming from. He looks on top of the manor but sees nothing. Only storm clouds, which fork with elegant lightning while rain falls in the distance but nothing major or out of place.

Did Anthony hear wrong? Paranoia can certainly cause tricks of the mind along with stress. It is quite possible that he misheard or imagined the sound...but Anthony is sure of what he heard. You cannot fake a scent or trick a trained ear.

"Let us go on a walk, Miss Alice," Anthony suggests. "We can walk to town. Are you up for the walk?"

Straightening her dress before staring up at him indignantly, she says, "Of course I can walk to town, Anthony. Shall I actually be walking or will you carry me again?"

Anthony cannot help but smile. "If you get tired, I will happily carry you, Miss Alice," he replies.

With that the two walk to town – perhaps a ten minute walk – and quickly made way through their errands. Alice secures a nice purple gown for the ball and her broach is perfect. Anthony temporarily parted with Alice during her dress fitting in search of manor help and found only another maid who proclaimed much

41

thanks for the job. After the dress fitting Anthony stayed very close to Alice. They had dinner at the local eatery and collected pastries from the bakery that Alice adores with all her heart.

As they are walking back Anthony has relaxed profusely knowing that the storm has passed. He no longer hears screeches or smells burnt flesh and blood. Alice happily snacks on her pastries only a step or two behind Anthony as she tells him about her trips into town with her mother and sometimes her father.

"Even though both Mother and Father did not like me having too many sweets," Alice tells him, "they always allowed me to stop by the bakery. I tried one of everything in there but these little puffs have always been my favorite."

Anthony chuckles as he watches her devour the pastries. "Why do you like those so much?" he asks. "One would think you would enjoy cakes much more, Miss Alice."

After a minute of silence, Alice replies, "The baker always gives me puffs with new fillings to try when I see him. Blueberry and strawberry, orange and chocolate! Yet I always go back to the original." She eats a few and licks cream off her fingers. "Cakes are good but to change one detail changes the whole dessert. At least these never change fully."

Although Anthony tries to ask her more about the pastries Alice refuses to speak anymore about her preferences. She continues to eat the puffs slowly as she is led back to the manor.

Suddenly a harsh wind blows carrying with it the scent of rain. Alice hugs the box of pastries close but one slip's from the box. When the wind dies down Alice bends to collect the pastry, hoping no dirt had marred its golden surface only to be saddened by the smudge of dirt on the puff.

Sighing, Alice throws the puff into the trash heap and takes a step towards Anthony who is now six or seven paces away from her when another stronger gust blows.

Sarah Gastright

Hands wrap around Alice's waist and she screams, dropping her box and thrashing around. Anthony turns around, his eyes suddenly wide with panic as he lunges towards the attacker who jumps out of his reach taking Alice.

"Get off of me!" Alice screams, landing a kick to her attacker's leg. Pain races up her leg as though she kicked stone and tries hitting it with her hand but to the same effect.

Anthony races to try and grab Alice as confusion and anger mix in his head. How had he not heard, not scented, the creature before this? If Alice is taken and harmed by the creature then his well-orchestrated plan will be for naught! Alice is only for Anthony, not for any hellish creature to take for a treat.

Then the creature cackles and, with the sound of metal being scratched with a nail, the creature's stony wings appear. Anthony curses the creature as he races to keep up with it. He knew of the creature but has not seen one for quite some time, since an old accomplice was imprisoned.

A gargoyle, the symbol of protection and power for humans, has only one goal: to become completely, truly alive. Most gargoyles are made of stone but come alive once they have absorbed enough feeling, transforming it into a strange stone-like life and then it cannot be sent back into a dormant state. How one could find Alice baffles Anthony since he had been sure that Alice's manor had no gargoyles before he came to serve her.

The gargoyle looks like someone took the body of a dog and placed a flat snarling cat's face on its head with ears of shriveled leaves and stony wings that look torn. Claws, which are thicker than a lion's, grip Alice's arms but feel eerily similar to fingers. Like all gargoyles the creature's eyes are fully red and glow like fire. He gives a yowl, sounding like a leopard and bear screaming at once.

Alice does not look afraid, only mad. Extremely mad for that matter. Probably more mad than Anthony had ever seen her before, and that is what he needs her to be.

"Prey," the creature screeches, "for the master. He pleasures my prey, he grants life. Demon, nay stop me. Prey es mine."

Anthony is quickly falling behind. Although the creature is made of stone it can still fly surprisingly fast and both Alice and Anthony can tell.

"Anthony!" Alice screeches when she realizes he is falling too far behind.

"Miss Alice," Anthony yells with his hands cupped over his mouth, "I will get you back. Be brave until then."

Something flickers in Alice's eyes and Anthony can tell she is not happy. What the emotion is he cannot discern but it is something that chills Anthony colder than knowing that Alice is being taken.

Alice feels her arms start to ache from being held. *What is holding me so tightly?* Alice wonders, angry that Anthony could not get her down. *No, what could possibly be* flying *and holding me so tightly?* Alice tries to struggle against the attacker's grasp but the creature only grips her arms tighter, causing pain to sear through her shoulders and upper arms.

"Put me down!" Alice yells, authority edging her voice.

"The master wishes you," the creature states. "Dropping you to splatter, not his wish."

"Why me?" she demands, thrashing her legs and twisting her body. "Why does your master want me?"

Another cackling fit from the creature. "Not my concern," the creature says. "Perhaps your bright Core? Maybe the master wants a new toy."

"You are doing his bidding blindly?" Alice asks, disgusted. "Following so foolhardily will only get you killed."

A screeching laughter emits from the creature and Alice cringes at the sound. "The master creates us, helps us live. The master is life. Why follow not?"

Angry, Alice lashes her hand out and hits the creature's stone body. She narrows her eyes at the stone feet, barely able to see the creature's claws on her arms. *A chunk of stone flying? Absurd*, Alice thinks. With the knowledge that Demons exist and roam around the Earth, it should not surprise her that a chunk of stone could fly, but it seems more unreal than Demons.

"Escape futile," the creature cackles. "Me talons strong than iron."

Clenching her teeth, Alice grates her fingers against its ankles, her skin tearing easily enough. Alice hisses from the mild pain, letting her hand float freely and listens as the creature taunts her with threats of eating her now. Despite her best efforts, Alice rolls her eyes and puffs out air, annoyed by the creature already.

As Alice watches the trees zip past, her eyes begin to droop and she is suddenly very tired.

"We about to pass barrier, human," the creature states. "Sleep, if you must. After the master claims you, rest not option."

Alice unwillingly falls asleep and something icy crawls through her mind, filling her sleep with horrible thoughts and dreams. She has not felt an emotion this strong nor as icy in years. Even though she sleeps, she is vaguely aware of all the sounds of creatures: the groaning, crying, screeching, clawing. Creatures that want her, yet Alice cannot figure out what they want with her.

Anthony, on the other hand, understands completely. It is the same reason why Alice summoned so many Demons simply with her hate, why so many tried to take her Core as soon as they found her, and why Anthony is so determined to protect her for his own needs. Alice is special in more ways than she can possibly imagine. If any other Demon gets his or her hand on Alice's Core, Anthony's plans will be ruined. Her Core has been crafted through the generations to be exceptionally powerful, so much so that it could possibly make a very powerful Demon even stronger than the current King.

Once Alice had been taken away from his sights, Anthony ran to the manor where he ordered the whole manor on lockdown. What Alice does not know about all the help in her manor is that most of them have previous military or a fighting background. Traits undesirable in your help but very useful for when Anthony must leave the manor with or without Alice inside. Anthony does not tell them everything; simply saying that Alice should be back in a few days and not to let anyone, under any circumstances, in the manor. Almost all the help could see how flustered and how irritated Anthony was as he issued the orders but they complied well enough. Anthony left soon after and picked up the scent of Alice's blood.

He smiles despite himself and the situation. "Miss Alice, your helpfulness could be what kills you before I can rescue you," he says to the sky. He follows the scent for a while, running as quickly as he can but his thoughts wander to dangerous territory. If Alice is dead – whether her Core taken or completely dead – then he would have to find a way to bring her back. Although someone can live without their Core, the body becomes a skeleton, a ghost of their former self, and completely useless to everyone else.

Then again, if Alice is not dead but, perhaps, had a change of heart, deciding to contract with another Demon then there would be more problems than anything Anthony would have the patience for would arise. It is possible but to do something like that would require massive amounts of energy to both break and recreate a contract, something no human could possibly accomplish. Their mind would be completely shattered, their emotions completely unstable. If any Demon would possibly consider that, it would be an easy way to gain a Core but it would take a long time of preparation. Alice is not the kind of girl to be swayed by many. After all, it was not like Alice automatically decided to pair with Anthony. She rejected his offer twice before deciding and grudgingly accepted. Of course, there were slight variables in the situation that Anthony may or may not have had a hand in but Alice has stayed faithful and true to her word and so has he.

Alice's scent grows weaker to Anthony. The scent of blood having faded leaving Anthony's mind to wander to other areas: Would she really form another contract? Is Alice stopping the bleeding herself, so he cannot find her as easily? *Perhaps she was attacked and now being dragged off,* he thinks. Anthony curses under his breath, wondering why he would think such absurd thoughts. Even though he comforts himself with his knowledge of his contract the thoughts still come.

Anthony curses profoundly when he comes upon a barrier. Alice's scent is extremely strong just past the barrier. Problem is, when Anthony contracted with Alice he was locked to this appearance and form, as to not stand out when he is with Alice. Demons that are contracted with humans are rarely ever allowed to pass through the barriers without permission from another creature inside the barriers. Humans cannot even come in barriers unless summoned and allowed access by an extremely powerful Demon. Obviously this was not a random picking. Someone wanted Alice specifically.

His thoughts cause another round of extremely loud curses. If anyone on the inside gave Anthony an entry ticket even though no one knows he is trying to get in, he would be slaughtered instantly. In this form he stands no chance against the fully-formed creatures and Demons inside at their peak power.

Hearing a sharp noise Anthony turns around to face a slender female Demon and, unfortunately for the both of them, they are well acquainted.

"Well now, what have we here?" she asks, a coy smirk on her face. "I would say the cat dragged you in, but it seems like you are chasing the gargoyle flock."

"Not the whole flock," Anthony replies, "just the one that took my contractor. I need her back."

"I hope you are not expecting me to let you in," she said.

"Serene, do not make this difficult," Anthony sighs.

Serene flips a lock of red streaked hair while crossing her arms defiantly. "It takes a difficult person to know another. I would get restarted if I let your through."

"Break the rules one time in your life and let me past the barriers."

"Why should I? You can get another person to contract with you as easily as a human kid can find candy."

"If I do not get in there and take my contractor back then we will both be killed." Anthony holds her eyes and sees her hesitating. "I am sure you know of Alice and I know you do not want the gatekeeper getting his hands on her Core."

Serene's red eyes narrow into dangerous slits as she judges Anthony. Once, a long time ago Anthony and Serene had been friends, allies in their goals. But time had worn their friendship thin and, due to some unfortunate circumstances Serene is now banished to watching over the barriers. A slap in the face to any Demon or creature.

Anthony knows that Serene is a Harpy, and she has been very successful in her training. When she decided to try and collect Cores, she excelled even quicker than Anthony, whose record of Cores surpassed most normal Demons. They met up and decided to hunt together and held successfully. Still, her true form scared off most people and made it troubling for their records, as Harpies have difficulties in masking their true appearances when threatened or angered. Regardless, she is quite pretty. Serene has platinum blond hair with streaks of red, making her hair appear almost white and her face is as pale as snow with eyes that glow like rubies. She could easily pass as a normal human except for her brittle bone structure. Her bones could easily snap when residing in her human form and her skin appears too small for her length, making her bones jut out as though starving. In comparison to a human, she is quite bewildering to behold. Due to one of many incidents with Anthony, she now strictly follows all the rules given to her – rarely bending them unless the situation absolutely calls for it.

"I will let you pass through," Serene says, her voice guarded, "on one condition."

"What is it?" Anthony demands.

Her red eyes flame in anger, far greater than what her calm voice suggests when she says, "Tell me why you killed them, my prey, before I could collect their Cores."

Chapter 4

Alice wakes up in a bed and, for a moment, her memories of what happened disappear and she buries her face into the pillows. She faintly catches an unfamiliar scent and the memories slam back to her. She bolts up and looks around. Not sure who but someone touches her cheek with a light touch and beckons her back down but Alice slaps the hand away.

"Feisty," says her captor. "Fitting really."

Turning to look down at him, Alice narrows her eyes before snarling, "You must be the master that my kidnapper could not stop talking about."

Smiling, he sits up and gazes steadily at Alice, who tries to suppress a shiver at the way he stares at her.

"Gargoyles are worse than a group of girls," he says with a shrug. "I am, indeed, their glorified master. It is a pleasure to meet you, Alice."

"How am I to address you?" *I am certainly not calling him 'the master' the whole time I am here,* Alice thinks vehemently.

"If I took on the face of someone you care for, would that be easier?" he asks. He covers his face with a hand and, when his hand moves away, her father's face is there. "Better? Or perhaps a female's would be better." A few seconds later, her mother's face appears.

Alice's hand lashes out but he grabs her wrist, holding it painfully tight. With Alice's mother's face, he bends in close and, using her mother's voice, whispers, "Slapping mommy is not allowed, Alice."

"My parents are dead and never coming back," Alice snarls, her eyes flaming in anger at her captor. "Learn of my history the next time you decide to kidnap me."

His smile twists oddly before her captor's face returns to normal and, with their faces close, Alice spits in his face. He recoils and Alice looks on smugly.

"Maybe we should start this over," he says tightly, wiping his face. "You can call me Chaos and I control almost every creature." An odd smile crawls on Chaos's face and he spreads his arms wide. "The gargoyle that came to get you was under my control just as every other creature you passed on the way here. That power resides even in my human form, believe it or not."

"You are not making sense," Alice tells him.

Chaos's grin grows wider as he climbs off the bed pulling Alice off as well. For a brief second, Alice glances down to see her clothes and blushes slightly. She is wearing an extremely thin black, knee length dress, all the proper places covered with thicker black cloth. Alice's dress ties around her neck, letting her arms and legs appear to glow in the strange light.

As for Chaos he wears black dress pants alone. His hair, black and hitting his chin, allows his completely black eyes to be seen in full view. His skin is almost translucent in the lighting and his touch makes Alice's skin crawl.

Soon Alice is dancing some strange dance to a song only Chaos can hear.

"Why do things need to make sense?" Chaos asks. "Why can they not just be nonsense? For that matter, what does it take for something to 'make sense'? Only the perspectives of what you silly humans discover and tell the young. If I told you that the sky was brown and the grass blue and that is all you knew, how would you know anything different?"

He spins Alice twice before bringing her in closely, leaning his face in. Alice glares at him, her gray eyes flashing like lightning and Chaos laughs at her, pushing her away an arm's length before twirling her and lifting her and tipping her.

"Things make sense so people can have sanity," Alice tells him. "If nothing ever made sense, if everything was nonsense, then the world would be insane."

Chaos laughs at her. "Oh, but what is the fun of being *sane*?" he asks. "If you are insane, nothing is impossible and you are limitless. No one bothers to tell an insane person that they cannot do something."

"They become a danger if they are told so," Alice argues.

"Idle-minded Alice, people only fear the unknown. Insanity embraces it." He pulls her in close, managing to twist her arms behind her. Alice glares at Chaos who smiles madly. His face leans in so that he feels her holding her breath. "Insanity embraces the unknown as I wish to embrace you, Alice."

Alice slams her foot into Chaos's shin. He pushes her away again, his dark eyes flaming, but his mad smile never leaves his face. Red dances in his eyes but Alice stands her ground, despite the icy monster trying to make its way forwards.

"Tell me if my guesses are right then," Alice says, lifting her head in defiance of him. "These barriers are places that humans cannot get into. Unseen, then, by humans?"

Chaos smirks. "Not unseen, just unwanted. Perhaps you disappeared into a mountain or a clump of shrubs. Humans cannot tell the barrier is there, but they unconsciously stray away."

"Then gargoyles are creatures that live inside barriers."

This time Chaos laughs. "All monsters and creatures originate in the human world. Humans are the greatest source of anger, after all, and they create more monsters than any Hell-tied Demon could possibly wish to. Not to say we cannot though."

"The gargoyle said you wanted me for my Core. My Core must be something special to be wanted so specifically by a Demon."

Chaos frowns, a confused and pondering look on his face. "You have lived with a Demon for a long time, according to my sources, but you know very little of these things. That is quite surprising." Chaos walks over to Alice and circles his arm around her waist and grabs her hand, preparing to dance again. "Who is your Demon, I wonder? He or she must be quite naive to believe their child is protected with ignorance."

Anger flames in Alice's chest, eager to beat the Demon down, but he starts dancing again and Alice is forced to make a quick decision.

"I do not know what you are talking about," she snarls. "I side with no Demons."

Another frown. "My gargoyle told me a Demon was spotted with you."

"That was my butler. He comes with me wherever I go." Perhaps Alice could bluff her way out of this. Then again, if he called her bluff, Alice would be backed into a corner and she is not certain how long she could last.

"Strange," Chaos muses. "Then you have no contract?"

"I have many contracts, as I run my family's business," Alice replies.

Chaos gives a small laugh. "Well then, I have my pure beauty made." He dips Alice low, low enough for her head to almost be touching the ground. "No contract, a feisty spirit, and a Core so much more powerful than that of any humans before." Chaos touches her chest, right below her rib cage and smiles madly. "You will be the treat I so desperately need."

He drops her on the floor and goes to leave. Alice sits up and Chaos smiles back at her.

"You are such a treat, Alice," Chaos states. "I wish we could have gotten to know each other."

With that he closes the door with a swish and Alice is left in the room to unleash her rage.

Spotting a vent, Alice gives a smile and starts scratching the top of her knuckles where she had rubbed her kidnapper. Biting her lip against the pain, she rubs her blood against the vent and then covers her hand. Hopefully the scent will travel to Anthony. After all, he had told her that he can always track her by the scent of her blood.

Alice lies on the bed and wraps herself up in a fetal position, trying to ignore the icy claws of a terrifying monster inside of her, wishing to hold her attention. For the first time in years, it shows its face and, just like last time, it shows at the worst of times.

Her body shakes and Alice closes her eyes tightly, burying her face into her knees as the cold and terrifying emotion crawls over her body.

Anthony swore I would never feel afraid again as long as I lived, Alice reminds herself. *How dare he let me be afraid now, of all times?*

Chapter 5

Anthony finally got inside the barrier. He temporarily lost Alice's scent due to the mix of other scents, but then he caught a brief wisp of Alice's blood. Short but strong, new. He follows her scent, dodging the creatures that lived there. Once or twice he was spotted by the creatures, but Anthony quickly destroyed them. Although he is significantly weaker in his human form he still holds enough power to rid the world of a few gargoyles and imps.

When he stumbles upon a mansion in the center of the barrier Anthony curses. He knows the owner of this mansion, although he greatly wishes he did not. He had hoped, with all his might that the gatekeeper would not be the one who took Alice. Anthony prepared for the worst.

Chaos, the gatekeeper of hellish creatures, one of the most powerful Demons in the world, lives inside that mansion. A long time ago Chaos was sealed inside a barrier, placed in his human form in hopes that his power would weaken but it only made him stronger. He gained full control over the creatures and would not hesitate to disintegrate someone that got in his way, no matter its race.

If Alice is really being held by Chaos, Anthony is not for sure who he should feel pity for. Although Alice can be a handful (especially if Chaos tries anything she does not agree to), Chaos is quite threatening on his own. He has no restrictions, no person to tell him what he can or cannot do. Chaos, in general, is simply threatening by his personality. Then again, Alice's personality….

Sighing, Anthony brings the real question front and center: Why would Chaos act now? There have been countless other storms in the years that he has been with Alice, so what makes now so special? Perhaps there is no reason and Chaos is simply choosing now to act. No, that feels wrong. Chaos may be abnormal but he always has a reason for all his acts.

Deciding to look around the house, Anthony gladly retreats into the shadows knowing that, in this form, he will be undetectable by Chaos.

Now, as for Alice, she is handling herself just fine. Her strange dress has been unchanged, but she has braided her pale blonde hair and washed her pale face. More than once creatures have come to take her to Chaos, but she told them to bring Chaos to her. After all, she is his guest this kind of treatment is disrespectful.

When Chaos did come, he certainly received his own earful about guest courtesy, which he listened to in bafflement. Chaos could not believe a human girl would dare lecture him on manners when she seemed to have so little of her own.

"From a girl with so little manners herself," Chaos says when Alice pauses for a breath, "I do not understand how you can lecture me on courtesy."

Glaring at him, Alice raises her head. "I am your guest," she reminds him sharply. "I am allowed to vocalize my complaints when I am upset inside of your home. As the host it is your job to absolve my vexes."

"This hardly seems fair," Chaos says with a sigh. "At least be a little more polite."

Snorting, Alice says, "I will show my manners when you express yours."

Chaos, baffled by the human girl, cannot even speak to his defense.

"Now!" Alice snaps. "What do you want from me?"

At first Chaos could not get the words to form.

"Well? Are you going to stare at me like a fish out of water?"

Clearing his throat, Chaos manages to say, "I would like to inform you that a meal has been prepared for you. I will escort you, if you would like."

"I refuse to leave my room," Alice replies simply.

Again Chaos is at a loss of words. "That is hardly polite! Come, the meal is wonderful."

Alice sits down on her bed, crossing her legs and arms before sending an icy glare to Chaos. "I refuse to eat outside this room. Bring your meal in here, if you wish, and we will eat in here. Otherwise: leave."

Chaos sits on the floor, puts his elbows on his knees, and his chin in his hands. He watches Alice carefully, taking her icy glare with ease. "Are you afraid of leaving the room?"

With a scowl, Alice snaps, "Never."

"Then why not come with me to the Dining Room? It is only a minute's walk from this room."

"As the guest, I do what makes me feel most comfortable." Alice raises her head in defiance. "You are holding the King's granddaughter in captivity and expect her to be simple? You expect her to respect her captor?" Alice laughs coldly once. "You are more dimwitted then Lord Edgar."

Seconds pass while the two stare each other down, Alice watching him with spite and Chaos with curiosity.

After a bit of silence, Chaos asks, "Who is Lord Edgar?"

Alice sighs in irritation. "What does it matter to you who he is?"

"Simple curiosity," Chaos replies. "Who is this Edgar and why do you call him dimwitted?"

Although his question takes Alice by surprise, she cannot think of any reason to not tell him. Alice also realizes that he probably will not stop asking until she finally confides. With a sigh, Alice states, "He is a silly Lord who tried to take the western lands of my territory and to make me marry his son. He believed me to be a pampered princess with little knowledge of anything. He certainly regrets thinking those vile thoughts now."

Chaos smiles at Alice, who glares in reply. Alice resents being unable to understand him and his smile, which has an odd happiness beneath it. Although she is only been with Chaos a short time, she feels like everything she says and does aids his plans.

"Well, if I cannot change your mind about eating in the Dining Room, perhaps I should just eat in here," Chaos says. He turns his head and two gargoyles appear. Alice tenses, glaring at the gargoyles that are standing outside her room. "Bring us our meal and a suitable table. Make it with haste, as to not disappoint our *royal* guest."

Quickly the creatures take heed to his order and bring food and a table in, setting it up in a flurry of movements. To Alice's surprise, the food looks completely normal, a spread of breakfast items including biscuits, eggs, and hash browns. Chaos quickly digs into his food but Alice stares at her plate as though expecting it to jump out at her.

When Chaos notices this, he says, "Alice, I am trapped in a human form, meaning I can only eat human foods. If I was going to poison you, I certainly would not put it in your food that I would be eating as well."

Alice had not thought of poison but of what the food would actually be. She had not heard nor smelled any chickens to lay the eggs, nor seen fields of wheat to make the biscuits. Then again, she had not done much investigating when coming into this strange place. Based on the area before she was brought here, Alice could not believe that the food would be made of normal things.

Still, Alice's mouth waters at the prospect of food. She has no idea how long she has been there and the last meal she can remember eating was dinner with Anthony and the pastries. Had Alice been asleep the whole night? A few hours? Perhaps longer? Either way, when her stomach growls, Alice takes a hesitant bite of the biscuit and her eyes widen in shock.

All her life no other breakfast could compare to her mother's. Still, this spread certainly rivaled that of her mother's cooking. Each item held rich flavor that surprised Alice more and more.

Chaos laughs at Alice's shock. "Have you not a good meal before, Alice?" he asks. "You seem very bewildered at the food."

"It tastes..." Alice searches for a correct word for a brief moment. "Exquisite." She blinks at the food on her plate. "You may have rivaled that of my mother's cooking."

Suddenly, gentle hands touch Alice's shoulders.

"How dare you say that about your mother's cooking, Alice?" whispers a kind voice.

Alice spins around and slaps Chaos, who now wears her mother's face. Despite his best efforts, Alice sees his black eyes on her mother's face and her anger flames.

"You *dare* impersonate my mother?" she snarls. "Not only are you disrespecting the dead, you are being rude to your guest. Now *sit* in your seat and be a *good* host."

Chaos chuckles, bringing his own face back, and holds Alice's chin between his thumb and pointer finger. Alice tenses at his touch and tries to jerk her face away. Chaos holds her face firmly and gives another chuckle at her.

"You should trust me, Alice," he says. "Have I done anything to make me not worth your trust?"

Alice snorts before saying, "Besides kidnapping me?"

Sarah Gastright

"Kidnapping is subjective," he says with a grin. "I like to think of it more as forceful visitation."

"I have no trust for you," she snarls in reply. "You have done nothing to earn my trust."

For a brief moment Alice catches him frowning but he carefully covers it with a half-smile, seeming merely bored with her. Still, Alice feels disturbed by his frown as though he threatened her. "I have prepared you a wonderful feast, free of poison," he reminds her. "I certainly have not harmed you physically as far as I know and I have respected your wishes. Is there more to your humanly trust than that?"

"When you try to build trust with someone, you should not kidnap them," she fires back. "Trust is not something you can build by simply preparing a meal, no matter how elegant."

Another frown, there for merely a second, and Alice feels her skin crawl. She dislikes the look of him frowning and she wonders if she has pressed her luck too far.

A few seconds pass and his frown reappears, deep and almost threatening. He moves away from Alice and walks to the center of the room. Chaos closes his eyes and turns around in a circle three times before going around the other way five more times. Then he stops, looking right at the vent. Alice sees his frown turn tight with anger as he walks towards it and sees the blood on the vent.

Before Alice can blink he is right in front of her, holding her wrists painfully at her sides. His eyes flash fire red, as though lit coals replaced his eyes. He yells at Alice, incoherent at first before seeming to yell real words at her.

"Why is your blood on the vent?" he demands his voice rising threateningly. "You said you had no ties with Demons. What logical reason would you have to put your blood on the vent?"

Raising her head in meek defiance, she says, "I was trying to find a way out, through the vent. My knuckles scratched the vent so I left it at that."

He shakes her hard and yells, "I do not believe you. There is no possible way to scratch yourself on the vent."

He takes her hands and brings them to his face. He focuses on her scratched hand and notes the rough scratches, something passing in his eyes that send icy claws through Alice's stomach, and then observes her other hand which has flecks of dried blood under the nails.

Chaos slaps Alice. She is so stunned from the blow, that she does not lift a hand in retaliation. Chaos pulls Alice up from her chair and then pushes her back. Alice's back hits the frame of the bed before she collapses on the ground.

"I planned on keeping you well," he snarls. "Keeping you happy and safe, just to be sure you were telling the truth. Now, Alice, now plans must be changed."

Fingers clench her face painfully and Alice stares right into his burning eyes, fueled by an unseen hatred beforehand.

"By the light of dawn tomorrow, you shall no longer be in existence," he snarls.

With that, he slams her against the frame again, causing specks to fill Alice's vision for a moment. She watches him walk out the room, the gargoyles moving the table and food away. She hears the sound of crashing and yelling, an uncontrolled rage blowing through the house like a storm.

After a minute or two Alice stands, her body shaking as fear fully engulfs her. It claws down her defenses against the irritating emotion as she crawls onto the bed, staring wide-eyed at the door and cringing at each loud thump.

Never once had Alice felt so feeble and scared in her life.

Chapter 6

By the time night has fallen, Anthony had scoured the perimeter of the house at least a dozen times and had figured out more than one way of escaping. He learned the rotations of creatures and their schedules. Not only that, but Anthony realized that as time passed he got angrier and angrier at his situation. Although Anthony knew what was happening outside the house, he could not figure out what was going on inside. Perhaps a trap for him or even a fake scent? True he had followed the scent all the way here but could they have led him on a false trail?

After some time, a gargoyle flies from the building and Anthony steps out in front of it managing to subdue it with a surprise ambush.

"The master will no allow this," hisses the creature to Anthony.

"Tell me what I need to know and you might live," Anthony growls in reply. "Is there a girl in there?"

Cackling, the creature stares at Anthony with malice. "Many girl seen. The master like toys."

Grabbing the creature's wing, Anthony gives a flick of his wrist and the wing is ripped clean off. A horrible scent of burning hair fills the air around them as a gooey black liquid trickles from the cracks. Obviously this gargoyle is slowly becoming a true living creature, much farther ahead than most around here. Anthony will not allow this thing to live.

"A girl, short, brought in earlier today," Anthony growls.

"The master no see us let," the gargoyle replies, pain fogging its voice. "Yes, girl come today, early, but I see no."

Anthony grabs the other wing and tightens his grip on it. "What is your master planning on doing with her?"

"The master say not," the gargoyle sputters. "Mention of her Core and blood, maybe. Very mad from girl. The room creatures claim—"

After a few moments a shriek breaks through the air followed by ringing silence. Gooey black liquid trails from the creature, its head and other wing tossed aside. Anthony's own rage boils high, knowing now that he has been wasting time while Alice has been trapped inside there. If Chaos is in rage, and Alice is the cause, then he would have to act fast. Still he knows that the guard shifts happen every hour and that would be his best chance at getting in undetected.

Anthony grits his teeth, knowing how much this could set things back. If Alice has learned anything that Anthony did not get a chance to tell her first, then things will certainly get tricky. Right now, all he can do is wait and hope that Alice can survive on her own for just a bit longer.

Within Alice's room Alice is thinking quite opposite things. Chaos came back soon after, his rage not totally quelled, and handed her a white dress. A white dress, reaching the floor with a slight poof from her waist down. He yanked her hair from the braid and then left. Alice, as soon as he left, started to panic. She paces and shakes, thoughts ricocheting around in her head. One after another, not stopping until she suddenly freezes and looks towards the wall. She tries to calm herself by taking in steady breaths and thinking. Using her mind instead of her nerves and emotions.

Alice knows that Chaos is going to try something that will not end well for her. Alice is assured that Anthony will get her in time, knowing he has yet to fail her and doubts he ever would. She also knows for certain that she and Anthony will be discussing many things when she gets back.

As for what she does not know…the list of question seems to continually pile up. Chaos's motives, what he is planning, why she is so important, why the sudden change in attire? Then comes questions for Anthony, who has told her so little of what the world truly holds. Gargoyles, coming to life? Barriers that humans subconsciously avoid? The existence of living gargoyles in general as well as other nightmarish creatures by the sound of it. What else could he possibly know that he has not told her?

Too much, Alice thinks. *I have put my bets on a painting I have not fully seen.*

Briefly, her mind flashes back to her contracting with Anthony. She had been frustrated beyond belief at her lessons and fled the house, escaping into the town and hiding whenever someone from the manor came close. By then she had refused Anthony's offer twice, refusing to even think of siding with something so crazy sounding in order to find the man who killed her family. Somehow, in Alice's frustration, she made her way to the graveyard, the only place in the town that made her nervous and sad. She walked in unafraid of what she would find. That time she was in over her head.

Three Demons laid in wait, hiding in the graveyard for someone to come along. Perhaps they had been planning to find and capture her, or perhaps she stumbled in under bad luck. Either way, they came after her and she ran. She was determined not to get caught by the creatures, but was unsure how to avoid it. She came to a resting point and it seemed that the Demons had not followed her, when Anthony appeared in front of her.

"I can protect you from this," he stated matter-of-factly. "Demons would not touch a contracted human as they are of no use to them."

"I can handle myself fine!" she snapped back, looking over her shoulder. "I lost them, anyways. You will blow my cover."

He gave her an amused smile, which only increased her irritation towards him.

"Have you ever seen a hunting dog abandon their game?" he asked simply.

Alice turned her head away from him. "Not once," she admitted.

"Demons are not that different."

As soon as he said it, the three Demons appeared, pouncing on her and knocking her off her feet. She fell with a thud several feet away, and cringed as she tried to stand. Somehow she managed to get up and run only a few more feet when another pounced, this time pinning her to a tree. She could not free herself and, when she looked up and saw Anthony's eyes gleaming down at her, she caved in and made the contract.

"I want to meet the man and discover why he would kill my family," she told him firmly, squirming under the grip of the crazy Demons. "Killing someone for a reason can be forgiven but cold blood can never be forgiven. What is it that you want in return?"

Chuckling, Anthony gave her a simple reply: "I want nothing more than to become the Demon King and you, Princess Alice Millersky, are the only one who can do that for me."

Clenching her teeth Alice felt the Demons surrounding her suddenly hiss in surprise and pain rushed through her arms and legs, beating around with pain from other injuries. After only a few heartbeats Alice was alone in the graveyard. Anthony appeared before her again, as she was walking out.

"We can discuss the details once you have rested, Miss Alice," he told her.

She sent him a glare. "*Princess* Alice."

"My mistake, Miss Alice."

Back in the present, Alice crosses her arms in a puff. She had forgotten how he had called her formally once, but had battled it ever since. She had forgotten how mad she remained at him for quite some time but the anger died to a low sizzle.

Sarah Gastright

All her anger that ever existed up until then seemed to just explode inside her head. She feels like she is drowning in a sea of anger. Her hands shake as she balls them into fists and she walks towards the bed frame, glaring at it as though it was the source of all her anger.

For a moment, Alice wants to yell and scream, throw something and smash it to pieces, but all she does is stare at the room surrounding her. Almost circular, she realizes, with no windows. A vent, a door and a bed were the only things indicating any possible room-like qualities. A door to where, though? Could it be unlocked or unguarded? Unlikely as Chaos had seemed rather livid. But perhaps he is too prideful to leave guards.

Attempting to quell her own anger she steps towards the door and tries the knob but to little success. She yanks the door hard but not even a budge. Pounding her fist against the door she yells out, demanding the door to be opened but no one replies, not even a whisper through the door. Perhaps they cannot hear her, though Alice doubts that. She continues to rage and yell, venting her anger in the only way possible. When she stops her hands hurt from hitting the unmoving door and her throat aches from all her yelling. She backs away from the door, shaking and panting, and attempts to control her never-ending flood of rage.

Eventually she crawls back onto the bed, as it is the only piece of furniture in the room, and stares at the ceiling. Anger unmatched in intensity still burns inside her body demanding to be let out, thirsting for a fight. No matter how much she tries it cannot calm down.

Somehow Alice eventually falls asleep and Chaos comes to check in on her, curious about her sudden spark in anger. His own anger still flames but Alice's makes his rage seem small, a candle next to a wild fire. He comes in and sees her scrunched up on the bed, her frame taut with an unknown anger.

Curiously, he crawls over to Alice moving to look her in the face as she sleeps. She murmurs something in her sleep and when

67

Chaos leans in closely he has to dodge a weak, half-hearted lash. He curses under his breath and glares at the child.

"Petulant being," he snarls. "Nothing good comes from your species except your Cores." Chaos grins but anger and pure madness taints his smile. "Even then, once I consume your Core, Alice, your species will be little more than a fly in my vision."

With that he abruptly turns and walks out the room, almost regretfully. He could feel the pure malice streaming off of Alice and he wanted more than anything to just take her Core then and there. Still, he refuses to take it without a proper ceremony first. He enjoys making things big and, for his glorious moment, he certainly will have things his way.

Outside the house, in the shadows, Alice is not the only one seething in anger. Anthony stands outside the house, within the shadows, festering and incubating his own temper. Even from the outside Anthony can still receive the faintest sense of Alice's outright rage, as could most other creatures around. Perhaps Anthony has been with her for too long, or perhaps he was only being hopeful, but he could almost feel the offset of her anger. Perhaps it stems from a different emotion, but Anthony pushes that thought away. As long as Alice could contain and retain that temper, she would be fine in the face of Chaos and could easily hold her own ground. Then again, by the way the guards are shuffling and grumbling he could imagine Alice had already done her fair share of aggravating.

Alice dreams of falling into a dark, bottomless pit. Anger tints the whole dream as voices reach out to her ears. It does not take long for the voices to remind her of the other emotions that thrive inside her. When she wakes up, her mind is a whirlwind. She focuses on regaining control over her rambunctious emotions, a task harder than what she remembers it being.

Chaos stands in a grand room as he directs the creatures on how to make the grand room even grander. His thoughts only briefly wander to the silly human resting in his spare room, wondering how her mind works. Although he enjoys spending time with the aggressive human, he cannot understand what makes her tick. None of the cogs in the clock are where they should be and he has no idea which part goes where. He simply wants the creature out of his life so he can begin anew.

Anthony sits in the shadows, concentrating very hard. He knows very well how the Demon King locks the Demons in their specific form and knows it is possible to temporarily unlock the seal. Anthony will have to spend much more energy than he normally would like to (especially when trying to stay concealed) and will not be able to regain more than a tenth of his power but it will be worth it. He compiles all his anger, all the anger he feels from Alice, until it becomes a key. He smiles darkly with his eyes closed, waiting.

Time slips through their fingers. Chaos is far too excited for the ceremony to take place while Anthony is restless for the key to open the lock just slightly. Alice, attempting to control her rampaging emotions, is unaware of the shift that all the creatures can feel. Chaos is blind to the shift. Perhaps this "shift" is too small to be seen or heard, but the feeling is perceivable, surprising and unsettling enough.

Now, before any creature can come within a few feet of Anthony they turn to a pile of goo.

"Perhaps," Anthony murmurs to himself, looking at the goo on his outstretched fingers, "I can afford to break another rule."

All three smile broadly: Alice for finally managing to secure her emotions and thoughts in place, Chaos for his completed preparations as he walks towards Alice's door, Anthony for obtaining the power he needs to crush those formally unbeatable.

Chapter 7

Alice is unaware of how long she spent both dozing and regaining control, or even how late it is, but she knows that when she jerks into alertness, something is different. She cannot see outside to tell the time of day, but Alice can feel the overwhelming silence around her long before she stirs from her restless dreams. Silence, thick and heavy in the air, as time slips carelessly by.

When Alice blinks to clear away a heavy grogginess she looks around the room and frowns. Nothing. Not a slither nor hiss, a whisper nor yell. No clattering of plates or cheerful words. She stands and moves across the room, aware of every creak and swish, each sound deafening in the silence around her.

Why are things so quiet? Alice wonders as she moves around the room on her tiptoes. She grabs a handful of her dress to lift it up slightly, hoping to prevent the swish but to little avail. Making her way slowly and quietly towards the door she presses a hand on it, squints as though confused, before pressing hard against it without a budge. Moving away as she decides it is still locked, Alice takes two steps back before, to her surprise, the door drifts open. Looking around the room, as though expecting someone to jump into view, Alice moves closer to the door and pokes her head out.

Nothing outside her door but the silence seems even more pressing. Stepping out into the hallway, Alice is surprised to feel that the floor is warm. Frowning, she quietly makes her way around the large house, expecting at any second a guard to drag her back to her cell.

No one comes and the silence is even more prominent. She is sure that some kind of trap will spring soon, alerting all the guards but no such thing comes. Alice follows the halls, allowing only one path for her to take. Did Chaos design his house this way or is he somehow manipulating the house? From what Alice has seen of Chaos she would not be surprised if the latter was true. If he is leading her, where to? She doubts an exit and would certainly be wary if she was suddenly brought to one, but she cannot think of where else he may take her.

Quietly, Alice walks seemingly forever. She tried to keep count of the turns but she eventually lost count, unable to concentrate on anything but finding where her path ends. Perhaps this is nothing more than a circle or square, leading her nowhere but back to her room. Maybe Chaos is bored and is playing a game on her, making her a mouse in his labyrinth house, only the scent of possible freedom to guide her way.

Eventually, Alice just stops in an extremely large hallway and turns around. Frowning, Alice sees her door is only a few feet away from her. Before she can move to go back hands grab her and a searing pain floods into her arm. Alice's eyes go wide and she opens her mouth to scream before her body falls over, limp as a doll.

From behind her someone grabs her waist and hoists her up, a high pitched laughter streaming from whoever holds her. Alice sees a flash of her attacker's face and a cold hand clutches her stomach then she is on his shoulder, her stomach pressing hard against his bony shoulder.

They walk around the house before coming to a large wooden door, one she would expect to see at a church, and her breath catches. She spots Chaos first, a spot of off-color in the room.

Everything is black, from the walls to the glass, the floor to the ceiling: everything is draped in the dark color. The area is like a gothic church: dark and yet oddly appealing. Candles light the walls and a large altar of dark gray sits above three steps with Chaos standing at one end. Her attacker carries Alice to him, switching her to now laying in his arms and, when Chaos grabs her, Alice wishes she could scream. His touch feels like burning ice to her skin and his smile suddenly more threatening and mad then what she has seen before.

Of course Chaos has changed for the event as well. A white dress shirt and pants, his hair neatly placed to stay from his face and now his eyes glow fully red, as though someone had placed fire on coals. Alice wants to fight him, to get away from him now but her body refuses to move.

"Thank you," Chaos says his voice tinted with something Alice cannot quite decipher. "You are dismissed, Imp."

From the corner of her eye, Alice sees the Imp bow, casting a jealous look towards Chaos, before leaving in a hurry.

"How do you like the paralysis potion I have made, Alice?" he asks, arranging Alice to hold her like a child. He chuckles to himself. "I will take it you are none too happy."

He moves her towards the altar, where the stone seems to radiate dark energy. A chill slithers through Alice when her ankle barely brushes the stone.

Dozens of candles erupt in bright light, brighter than what Alice expected and Chaos laughs darkly. He places Alice slightly above the ground and she is held there, barely two inches from the ground with her head kept straight and her arms behind her back.

Chaos brushes his hand right below her rib cage, right at her sternum, and he sighs in some form of bliss.

"It is quite sad, Alice," he muses. "This could have been avoided, really, if you would have been more willing." He taps his fingers across her chest, icy fire burning her to the very core at the slight tap of his fingers through her dress. "You would be safe and protected here, Alice. All you could possibly desire at your command." This time, Alice feels something sharper brush her skin, a slight prick on the skin. Not enough to draw blood but enough to know that, whatever he is tapping against her dress, it is sharp. "If you had told me to begin with that you were in a contract...well, things would not have to end this way." He smiles and Alice can see, just barely, a dark feather appear right in front of his head.

A tearing sound meets Alice's ears and the icy fear escalates to a painful burn. Every single form of panic slashes across Alice. All Alice's senses scream for her to just run, escape, hide. Once, long ago, she had followed those senses and maybe they had aided her then. Now all they do is amplify her panic, allow every sense to intensify beyond her normal abilities.

Chaos waves the feather in front of Alice's face with a hungry smile on his face.

"I am not one for long speeches," he tells her, "but I must say how lucky I am to have taken this when I could. It certainly makes for convenience."

From some long forgotten part of her mind Alice recognizes the feather as a quill. It was one of the quilled pens her parents would use when she would study music, as they would show her what a conductor would do for certain songs and how they kept time. Only with her parents, the feather was white, well-worn and very much a writing tool.

"Perhaps it was not one of the best deals made for the owner," he informs Alice, "but it works wonders, does it not?"

With a brisk shake, the feather turns a stunning white, a white radiance seeming to flow off of it. Then Alice hears Chaos hum a song and the feather seems to pulse in time. After a few moments, Alice recognizes the song, one of her favorite pieces to have played. One of her mother's, one that was only to be performed at night, so she had always been told. Of course, Alice had heard her mother play it on her own instrument but Alice had only been able to successfully play it once or twice.

Pain ripples in Alice's chest, breaking the brief revere. Now an insistent dark melody screams in Alice's ears, amplified by the church's acoustics. Alice knew the song, but could no longer place it. It no longer holds the same melody, tune or tempo of her mother's song. Chaos hums the song, the feather still pulsing in beat but now pain sears in Alice's chest.

"Once you are gone, the world is mine."

Fire and ice, burning hotter and colder than anything she has ever felt, Alice feels herself slipping, unable to stay afloat. Pain rolls in waves, intensifying as the feather pulses, the dark melody thrumming in her ears seeming duller and duller.

Alice's eyes flutter briefly, unable to beat the paralysis as Alice slips in and out of consciousness. Chaos smiles madly, hoping to prolong the pain for the irritating human girl. He is careful though, as too much of any emotion in this stage could be disastrous.

Without Chaos's knowledge, a single drop of Alice's blood hits the ground. A drop of blood in a bloodless ceremony. Ignorant of the drop, he grips the Core within his hand and, preparing to yank out the object, he hears what sounds like a single drop of liquid in an empty, watery cave after a second of the splattered drop.

Releasing his grip, for barely a moment on Alice's Core, he does not get a chance to register his unwanted guest before he is thrown across the gothic church, slamming against the black walls. Stunned, Chaos does not move for a moment and his guest takes the opportunity.

Moving in a blur of motion, Chaos's guest appears in front of him, anger and cold hatred radiating off of him as he grabs Chaos and throws him through the dark glass of the church. He hears Alice slump to the ground, a soft swish as the material of the dress bunch together. Moving towards her, he sees her eyes come into focus and he smiles.

"Hello Miss Alice," he says kindly. "Rest here for now. I will be back in a moment."

Placing her carefully away from anything, Anthony turns towards the shattered window and sees Chaos frowning in the frame of what used to hold thick glass.

"Why does it not surprise me that you are the one who contracted with Alice," Chaos states plainly. "Regardless, you will die painfully."

For a moment, Anthony does not seem to notice Chaos moving but Anthony quickly catches Chaos by the collar, Anthony's eyes burning brighter and angrier than Chaos's eyes of fire.

"You do not seem to realize how much trouble this has been," Anthony states just as plainly. "Miss Alice will now be disastrously behind in studies and she has missed numerous meetings. I would appreciate it if you would just let me leave with her."

Chaos has never once been stunned by a Demon's words but the plainness of Anthony's behavior baffles him. He had expected a fight, vile words, even to have to get his own hands dirty. Never once did it cross his mind that Alice's contracted Demon would simply ask for her to leave.

"I must decline," Chaos says after a minute. "Alice is my prize now."

Anthony grabs Chaos by the arm, twisting the shoulder to the point where a loud crack resounds in the church. Chaos yells in pain and glares at Anthony.

"You have the life, power, and appearance of a Demon," Anthony reminds him, "but you are stuck in a human form. Do you know what that means, Chaos?"

"Yes," Chaos snarls, "but I refuse to let you."

Faster than expected Chaos lashes out, slashing brutal claws threw the air and tearing the flesh open on Anthony's face and neck. For a moment, blood pours from the lethal wounds but they heal up soon after. Chaos looks on in mortified confusion.

"Within a barrier, most Demons cannot expose their true form if they are contracted with another species. Of course, that rule applies if a Demon can get inside of a barrier once contracted which is nearly impossible. As such, their demonic power is cut off and is restricted to the base line that was set long ago." Anthony takes a step forward and, when Chaos lashes out again, manages to grab hold of the Demon's hand and bend it backwards. "That is the rule all Demons abide by, in order to keep peace and stability. It is only fair, after all, for a Demon to stay human with a human contractor." Chaos cringes faintly as Anthony presses his wrist farther and farther back. "It is a rule set in paper, one of minor punishment and a punishment I am willing to endure if I get Alice back."

Chaos lashes out with his legs, causing Anthony to release his grip and stumble backwards. Glaring at the unwanted guest, Chaos curses him and, at the sound of raised voices, Imps and gargoyles stream in along with hobgoblins and many other species with flaming pelts. All of them start to rush towards Anthony but almost instantly the creatures turn to black goo.

"We had a deal, Chaos," Anthony says to Chaos, ignoring the rain of black goo. "Perhaps you have forgotten in your age of the deal and the power in which I wield when allowed to express even a tenth of my true power. I know your extent quite well."

Gritting his teeth, Chaos thinks quickly and then smiles wide and unnerving at Anthony. He stands up, swaying a bit against the flood of pain, pain which he has never felt before.

"Perhaps I have forgotten in my age," Chaos tells him, "but have you forgotten what you have done in the past? All the vile rules you have broken? A slip of the tongue could easily land you in the same position as I." Chaos looks over Anthony's shoulder and smiles widely.

Anthony starts to reply but then he follows Chaos's line of sight which leads to the spot where Alice used to lie. Looking back over to Chaos he sees an Imp holding Alice on his shoulder and glowering at Chaos.

"You have gained tremendous power in the time that we have been apart," Chaos admits. "Regardless, you are still no match for the power I control. You had your chance for surprise but you have lost it, along with your chance to have Alice." His eyes flame as the smile on his face grows tinted with pure madness. "If I cannot have Alice's Core, vile and unwanted guest, then you certainly cannot have her Core either."

Slowly, the Imp turns around and shows Anthony Alice's wide eyes, unable to blink as the paralysis still flows through her body. At first, Anthony does not understand what he is saying but then a hobgoblin appears. His green skin and lumbering body pulsing with unused strength as he carries his giant club.

As soon as Anthony takes a single step towards her Chaos appears in front of him, sending another lash with his claws, this time at Anthony's legs. Both men cringe but only Anthony kneels, his muscles torn.

"Snap her neck, hobgoblin!" Chaos screeches in joy and madness. "Let her death be the end of this battle and I be the winner."

A few more lumbering steps and the hobgoblin places his club on the ground with a thud. Anthony can see the flicker of fear in Alice's eyes as she stares at the hobgoblin but then she turns to look at him. Instantly that fear switches to disgust and anger.

Chaos laughs loudly, his eyes wide and he sends another slash towards Anthony's back, but Anthony is only vaguely aware of it. All he can see is the disgust, the pure anger, towards him and for some reason Anthony feels a smile creep on his face, the smile he always wears around Alice. Anthony's body trembles as another, more vicious slash rakes across his back. Still, Anthony's smile does not leave his face and, after a moment, he pushes Chaos to the side.

His body stitches itself back together, mending with a sudden snip of pain, the cause of multiple fatal wounds. Chaos glares at him and as the hobgoblin grabs Alice's head, Chaos grabbing Anthony's neck with his long claws, the two stare at each other intently for a moment before Anthony closes his eyes.

Perhaps a second after he closed his eyes Anthony feels a vibration, calm and frightening and when he looks over at Alice he sees the glare she sends his way. He sees that her mouth is closed more comfortably now and he notices her blinking once or twice, although slowly, as though exhaustion makes it difficult to keep her eyes open. If anything, she appears tired now, but she hums the song beautifully.

Both the Imp and hobgoblin screech and run out the room, dropping Alice in their retreat, and Chaos stumbles backwards, looking pained and suddenly tortured.

"She never learned the song," he snarls. "I made sure of it! I made sure that precious violin was smashed to pieces!"

"Humans are peculiar things," Anthony states, still smiling at Alice, who lies on the floor, her fingers twitching. "When you think you have them figured out, something changes and then they are a whole new species."

"You must have taught her the song," Chaos accuses.

Not even looking at Chaos, Anthony walks towards Alice. He is surprised at how uncomfortable he feels as he approaches her. Is it her anger that makes him so uncomfortable, or the song? Regardless, he reaches her and helps her into a sitting position. Her eyes dart to him, the glare only intensifying the strength of the song. Anthony chuckles.

"Perhaps you did not know this, Chaos," Anthony tells him, his back still turned away from Chaos, "but, by the time I reached her, the violin was already gone. She would not touch an instrument, no matter how much people begged of her. I would never been able to teach her the song."

Lifting Alice up, he walks over to Chaos who has fallen to the floor, writhing in some pain Anthony could not understand.

"I can gather that this will not be the last time we see each other," Anthony states plainly. "Please try to schedule a time when it is more convenient for both parties."

With that, Anthony walks out the church, no creatures daring to come within ten yards of him, and Alice falls silent, her breathing leveling out. Anthony chuckles at Alice, feeling her head droop as she falls into a peaceful sleep. Anthony walks out the barrier, appearing at the gates of Alice's manor and he smiles again.

Alice grabs hold on his torn shirt, causing Anthony to look down to her, and, in a groggy voice murmurs, "We have much to discuss, Anthony."

Dread replaces the feeling of peace Anthony had built up. Of course she must have heard him mention the deal to Chaos and her experience must have brought questions to her mind. Still, Anthony wishes that he could have more time to make up something believable. Alice slumps back against his chest just as they cross the threshold of her manor and much of the help come running up.

Once she is settled in bed, Anthony gives them a half true rundown of the events and discovers information that only they could know. How long they had been gone, what the weather had been like, how the people in town had reacted, and how much their schedule has been ruined. Anthony demands that guards be posted around the windows of Alice's room and outside all doors. The help is happy to comply, and Anthony could see the sudden wave of relief in all their faces to have Alice home safely and unharmed.

Anthony retreats to his study, where he tries to straighten everything out in his head. Years of planning, of carefully orchestrating events and her safety, now turned to little more than dust. Should Anthony say the wrong thing at the wrong time, bring up a subject with the wrong ending, all will be lost and much will be ruined. He had lost Serene's trust that way and he would not allow the same to happen with Alice. He could delude her for a bit, sate desire for knowledge for now as he tries to find the time to explain things rationally to her.

Miss Alice

They had been gone nearly three months in the human world but barely a day had passed in the barrier, merely hours to those inside of it. Anthony knew that Alice sleeping so much is both a side-effect of the paralytic venom and time lag.

By the time dinner arrived, Anthony had made a bare plan of what to say and what not to, to ask his questions once he had gained a step above her. Anthony asked a maid as she passed, much more politely then he had in the past, to bring his and Alice's meal to Alice's room. She complied and soon after a cart appears with plates of food. Anthony thanks her and takes the food on his own to Alice's room.

She is sitting up when he opens the door, staring out a window at the darkening sky, a kind smile on her face. He had changed her from the white dress to a large shirt that had been at the bottom of her dresser, possibly her father's, and he could not help but notice her knuckles, now scabbed over, wondering if he should bandage them. As soon as he entered the room, her head swiveled to him, glaring at him as he came inside the room.

"I wish not to eat with you," she hisses. "You disappoint me."

For some reason, the words sting Anthony. "Miss Alice, I am afraid that I so not quite understand," he says, confusion tainting his voice. "Something I have done has disappointed you?" Anthony had not expected a thank you from Alice, rather for her to revert back to her normal routines and possibly a lecture.

Moving off the bed, her large shirt reaching barely to the middle of her thigh, Alice creeps towards him, using little support of her bed and simply her own willpower. For her to be up, so soon after experiencing the paralytic from an insane Demon within a barrier, Anthony is certainly surprised – and more than a little proud.

She comes right up in front of him, staring up at him with lashing gray eyes. "You have lied to me, Anthony," she snaps. "You have not only lied but you have broken a promise I thought you swore to never break. Either you are to get far from my sight or I will have you removed from my manor."

When Alice sways Anthony naturally goes to balance her but she slaps his hand away, her scabbed over knuckles reopening as she balls her hands into fists, and a slow stream of blood trickles down her hand. She simply glares at him her body swaying a bit and Anthony cannot tell if her shaking hands are from anger or from another emotion that he cannot quite place. Not fear, certainly not now, but something much more... contradictory to what he could see in Alice's mind.

Still, he blinks at her, not quite comprehending. "Miss Alice, I do not recall ever breaking a promise nor lying to you," he states. "Tell me what I have done, Miss Alice."

Alice looks behind him, sees the door is still open and shoves him, with all her might, out the door, pushing the cart out with him. Anthony is stunned at Alice's actions, unable to grasp where this sudden malice is stemming from.

"Once you have figured it out, come talk to me," she snarls. "Until then, stay out of my sight."

She slams the door, and Anthony hears the lock click into place. Although he could still break the door, the remaining wisps of his power still lingering, he is too shocked to actually act upon the thought.

He beats on the door with the side of his fist. "Miss Alice, open this door," he orders. He pounds more insistently. "Miss Alice, at least eat. You are weak and the paralytic could still cause damage if you do not give yourself energy. Miss Alice, open the door."

Through the door, he can hear her drawing the curtains closed, hear her stumble around the room, her legs still weak and her body trying to shake off the paralytic, and when she hits the bed, he hears something from Alice he had never heard before.

His beatings stop and he merely looks at the door. "Miss Alice, I do not understand what I have done to upset you," he whispers into the door, "but if that is your true desire, you will not see another hair of me until I have figured it out." He turns away from the door and sees a maid scurrying around.

"Mister Anthony?" she asks and then notices the cart behind him. "Is something the matter?"

"Alice wishes to be alone right now," Anthony replies tightly.

In the time it takes for the maid to look in the direction of Alice's bedroom and back, Anthony has disappeared.

Chapter 8

Three weeks passed and Alice quickly regained strength and composure. She now walks around the house as proud as before and orchestrates her own meetings well enough. Anthony has kept true to his word, staying clear of Alice's sight although she knows he stills stays around the manor, as work is still done on time and with accuracy. Every now and again Alice will see him in the corner of her eye but ignores it. Alice still holds firm to her convictions and he has yet to break it, after all.

Alice quickly readjusted to her life back in her manor: setting up meetings and lessons, following through with both (although some more grudgingly then others), while still running errands all around town. She spends a great deal of time in the library researching multiple topics, most of which revolve around the creatures she saw during her time within the barrier. Still she has come up empty handed and knows the only way to get those answers is to ask Anthony. To that thought – usually appearing at the library – she snorts and leaves for her manor.

As for her lessons, Sir Smith noticed her sudden interest in the kingdom's defenses and her patch of land's well-being. Seeing as she holds very little power over her patch of land, he worries not for her area but for the sudden chill to her demeanor, how that will affect the kingdom as a whole. He comes down at least three times a week, staying for long hours and worries greatly for Alice but she pushes him away, deciding not to concern him.

Lady Belle returned with lectures upon lectures, coming twice a week to catch up on lost time. Alice agreed to pick up an instrument again and, when the King caught wind, he sent an old violin from the Castle just for her. Although Lady Belle had already bought Alice a violin, Alice became immediately attached with the old instrument. Although Alice's stubborn behavior towards Lady Belle has changed little, Lady Belle is smug about Alice's sudden cooperation, quiet mouth, and sudden change in eagerness to learn how to be a proper lady.

Much of the help notices Alice's disappearances from the manor during her free days, her late return and her disappearances to the garden. With three doctors on hand at all time Alice always has someone fussing over her. Two of the doctors fuss over Alice, telling her that after such an ordeal she should stay inside and rest when she can while the other doctor tells them to let her have her space, as she needs as much space as they could possibly give.

All the cooks notice her decreased interest in eating her full meals, instead taking to her studies rapidly. All the help revel in hearing her play in the mornings and the late night but a few wonder if she actually sleeps. Some nights Alice is unable to get a wink of sleep no matter what she tries.

Alice lets none of them come in close to her. Not from what she experienced in the barrier, but because their need to stay close to her is bothersome. After she came back, they pestered her for information, babied her as though she was a cracked vase about to fall. Smothered her in words and opinions. Even though she knows that they are doing this for her best interest and perhaps Anthony's orders, she still refuses to admit that any codling is good for her.

A few days back Alice received word that her Grandfather would be coming to stay for a night before he continues on his tour of his kingdom. Alice, of course, doubts that is his only motive to come to the manor now when he has not visited Alice in years, but she told him that the manor would be prepared for his visit and his guards and horses. Alice expects him later in the current day and expects him to stay two nights, despite his decree of only staying one.

So, as Alice sits in her Show Room, meeting with a Lord who wishes to form a trade agreement with her, Alice wants to be anywhere but there.

Perhaps the Lord thinks her unaware of the trade routes in her territory. He wants to set routes right between the neutral villages to her southeast. They are not exceedingly powerful but

Sarah Gastright

they have great knowledge of the land there and Alice already has trade agreements with them for medicine in exchange of other goods. They do not like having the King's soldiers in their villages, creating tension along the borders but Alice has managed to keep brittle peace between them well enough, offering protection from this Lord's armies. Unsurprisingly he wants to station his men there ("Yours too, Princess, just for safety and surveillance, of course.") but Alice declines that declaration. Farther to the south, there is a river which floods after harsh winters which connect the two borders much better and go through the King's territory. Also not to Alice's surprise, he does not like the idea, as his territory has strained relationships with the King.

After nearly three hours of bickering Alice stands up, straightening her skirt of her dress, and stares at him.

"Lord Raymond," she says, voice firm, "please explain to me why you wish so badly to go through the southeast territory when the southern territory is much closer."

Standing quickly, the Lord stares at Alice with barely-present innocence. "Princess Alice, the town already has trade routes set in play," he informs her. "If we want to go from the south we would have to build bridges and roads, set up guards... The time and cost would far exceed that of the southeast route."

"Do you believe me dumb?" Alice asks him.

He blinks before saying, "Not at all."

"Then why pester me with this nonsense?" she asks. "I know your tension with the King – I know of it well, Lord Raymond – and I also am aware of your *disagreements* with the territory in the southeast." She narrows her gray eyes at him and sees him look away. "So, Lord Raymond, why not try my question again. Why are you so insistent that we go through the southeast territory?"

For a moment, nothing is said and Alice decides to jump on his silence.

"I would certainly like to have trade between the countries," she tells him honestly. "Not only would it help the common people but trading with you would help my Grandfather's military as well as my own military. In order for this agreement to go through, I must know of your intentions."

85

More hesitation but Alice can see that he has accepted her honesty. Walking over to a drawer, she grabs a map and brings it to the table, showing the territories. Pointing to her own area, she speaks to him carefully, informing him that her supply of metals – such as steel and iron – has never been all too good, to say the least, and having those basic metals would certainly help improve the technology in her territory. If her technology increased then the Lord would have a strong ally on his side, increasing his territory's power as well.

"Of course," she tells him, "if the territory in the southeast were to see us trading metals such as those, what would they think? Simple trading, no doubt." Alice rolls her eyes as she makes the sarcastic remark. "They would assume we were planning a war, Lord Raymond. Having a war against them would certainly put a damper on the brittle peace I have tactfully built up. Now, if we traded from the south, since I can personally convince my Grandfather to allow the trade, things would go smoother and the bridges would be unneeded if we can build the correct boat."

After a few moments of considering, the Lord gives a single laugh, closing his eyes for a few seconds before staring right at Alice.

"I believe you have won," he says.

Smiling, Alice says with a dangerous smile, "I believe this is my checkmate."

Sighing, he says, "If you must know, I was hoping to spark a bit more trust within the territory in the southeast. We have been bitter enemies for many years and, should we get trade between both of the territories, the profits would increase in all three countries."

He goes on to tell Alice about the profits that could be made and the alliances that could be forged, but Alice sees him clearly through the whole thing. He reiterates the wish of peace too much, hurriedly talks about the possibilities of any war and would not look directly at Alice during the talks of trading metals to the southeast territory.

Eventually, he pauses for a breath and carefully meets Alice's gaze. Instantly he recoils. Alice sits in her chair, head leaning on her hand, legs crossed, and a very unhappy look on her face.

"I was told once that all liars share the same attribute while talking," she informs him. "Being as young as I am, many Lords come to my manor wanting separate things. Trade, alliances, treaties, land, even courtship, and almost all of them suffer one of many fatal flaws." Her eyes narrow into dangerous slits. "Can you guess what those flaws would be?"

He starts to stammer out possible things and, after a handful of minutes, Alice raises her hand and stands up. She sees him reach towards him waist but Alice simply smiles.

"Firstly, they overuse the formalities," she informs him, "especially when they want something they know I am unwilling to give." Alice takes a step towards him. With only ten steps from her to him, she would have to work quickly. "Secondly, they refuse to meet my eyes during a lie. That one baffles me most of all, as it is the most common way to tell a liar." As she spoke, Alice managed three steps and he brings out his revolver, placing five bullets inside his barrel before pointing it at her head. "Thirdly, they always come armed."

Another few steps and he yell's out curses, yelling things that should hurt her but simply glide away from her skin. She notices the craftsmanship on the gun, noting the older appearance but sturdy frame. New, but made to look old, a beautiful piece of work. She notices the five spaces for bullets and notices that the bullets are hidden from her view. Alice is not a fan of guns but she learned plenty about guns as part of her years of education and training. She is very aware of the rarity of his gun.

With the gun placed squarely between her eyes, Alice looks up at Lord Raymond with the most threatening smirk she could possibly muster.

"Before I say the last give away," she tells him, "let me inform you of something you will find useful. All of my help knows of you being here as well as my Grandfather. Within the hours, he will be here and he will know who has slain me. So, with this, you have two options."

"What are they?" demands Lord Raymond, looking around the room.

"One, you shoot me and risk the punishment of the King and numerous unnamed people," Alice states, "or two, you could put the gun down, leave my manor, and never show hide nor hair around here again unless you want to come with an honest reason to trade with me."

After a moment, Alice sees him hesitating but, to Alice's surprise, he asks, "What was my give away?"

Smiling, Alice whispers, "You hesitated."

He opens his mouth to speak but the butt of a gun smacks on his head and he crumples. Alice picks up the gun, unloads it and kicks it across the room, falling into her chair with a sigh.

"Another failed meeting, Princess?" asks her current guard.

"Sadly, yes," she replies, sighing again. "To think that I really hoped Lord Raymond would give an honest trade. We do need the metals, but I guess there will be others."

Her guard smiles grimly and pulls him out into the hall before calling for extra assistance. Alice hears people shuffling their feet. She strains to hear one voice and, when she does, Alice smiles, leaning her head once again on her hand. Alice had ordered him out of her sight but she had picked up on what he did to stay away from her sight. For instance, she knows he brings her breakfast because it is always in her room in the morning with no one around. She also knows how he stays outside the Show Room whenever she has someone coming for a meeting. She sees him briefly in the corner of her eyes when she goes into town. He certainly goes to great lengths to avoid being seen but to confirm her safety.

Alice finds the game amusing. Hide and seek with a shadow at night. There, but hidden too well. A hider of great skill, a seeker unable to break the game. How long until one of them caves? Knowing in her gut that she would not be the first, and wanting Anthony to admit himself wrong. To discover this on his own, but also curious for information. When he brought her back she had wanted more than anything to know the answer to her questions but she had been left alone for too long to think on her own.

Perhaps she acted rashly but that does not mean she will back down. Anthony is at fault and that is the end of it.

A knock on the door brings Alice from her thoughts. A maid pokes her head in and smiles nicely. "Your grandfather and his men have arrived, Princess Alice," she says.

Nodding, Alice stands. "Thank you. I will be there with haste."

With a bouncing nod, the maid scurries from the room and Alice takes the gun and bullets from the floor and places them in a drawer with ten or so other guns already inside. Taking one last glance at the orange sky, Alice turns and hurries down the hallway, placing an excited smile on her face.

For a moment, just as she rounds a corner, a flash of black passes through her vision and something slips into her hand. Stopping, she turns around and looks around the corner but she sees no sign of Anthony down either hallway. A small, square piece of paper rests in her hands. She unfolds the paper, prepared to read it, when the bellowing voice of her Grandfather reaches her ears first. Turning her head up, flashing a smile of false warmth, she rushes to her Grandfather.

"You have grown since I last saw you, my dear!" the King bellows with a laugh. "Not much though, I am afraid."

"I was nine the last time you saw me," Alice reminds him carefully, allowing a short laugh to please him. "How are you fairing, Grandfather?"

He smiles at Alice, his gray hair kept close to his head, though his face shows no sign of age. Alice, as a child, had always wondered what the King really had to do, as it seemed her parents did all the work themselves. When Alice first met the man, he had no sign of old age save his hair, while her father had already started to wrinkle from stress. Strange, really, that the ruler of a kingdom has little signs of age while the ruler of a small portion of the kingdom shows beyond his years in age.

"And in those missed years you have matured into a fine young Queen," he tells her and engulfs her in a hug. "I have heard from Lady Belle and Sir Smith of your vast improvements. With your sickness, I feared the worst but it appears that you have recovered well."

For a moment Alice forgets about her false story and almost questions him but catches herself quickly. Although her help was told of Alice being kidnapped, they knew little of the true story and Alice had little to tell them. In order to keep peace around the King and other countries, she informed her teachers that she had fallen ill and they reported back to the King of her illness. Of course, she fabricated much, and an illness that kept her out of touch and unable to learn for three months surely made them question, but Alice was able to handle it with ease. As her recovery from the paralytic had been slower than she had hoped, her story of being weak even after the illness had passed surely helped.

"A mere illness made of unintelligent beings cannot push me over, Grandfather," she tells him, giving him a frail hug in return. Curiosity pulls at the back of her mind about the paper and she attempts to sneak a look at the paper when her Grandfather breaks the embrace and grins at her, pride shining in his eyes.

"I hear that you are following in your mother's footsteps," he says.

"Sir?" she asks, confused.

"Lady Belle has told me that you seem to be a prodigy with your violin," he tells her with a laugh. "Of course, I knew you were gifted but to hear you be called a prodigy is certainly amusing. Although, I am curious to your sudden leap into your studies again." He looks around, as though searching for someone. When he looks at Alice again, his jovial blue eyes meeting her curious gray eyes, he laughs for a moment. "Where is that butler of yours, Alice? Last I saw of you, the two could barely be apart."

Sniffing harshly, Alice simply says, "We had a brief disagreement and I sent him on leave to think of his words." When she pauses she sees her Grandfather start to build a question and decides to change the subject. "Grandfather, you must be weary from your travels. Come, a meal has been prepared for your arrival." Looking over his shoulder, she gestures towards the guards as well. "You as well. All guests within my manor will be fed and cared for equally."

Alice catches their surprise but leads them towards her Dining Room where, as soon as everyone is seated, food is placed in front of them and the guards start to inhale the food and chat amongst themselves. Alice and the King eat properly and with amused smiles at the guards.

Eventually, once the guards have drunk their share of wine and the King appearing tired, Alice decides to ask him of a favor rather unladylike.

Moving in close, she says, "Grandfather, this may be an odd request from a Princess but I would like to go hunting with you one day."

He chokes on his wine, sputtering and coughing, careful not to draw attention when he turns his head to look at Alice, his face and eyes showing his instantaneous refusal before he can utter the syllables.

"A Princess in your situation should not be bothered with such brutish and trivial things!" he scolds. "Perhaps should other heirs be about, possibly, but with only you, after your long illness, I would never consider the option. What has inspired the sudden, foolish desire?"

Grabbing her own cup and taking a steady drink from her diluted wine (Alice has never been fond of the taste of wine and prefers to keep her head in many situations), Alice watches her Grandfather carefully, judging her next words with caution.

"My father and you used to hunt," she eventually says calmly. "A time of bonding, perhaps, between the to-be King and current King, and at the time I would never consider such options." Casting a glance at her Grandfather, she sighs. "You see, as having neither brothers nor uncles, I know little of hunting and what it can hold. From what I remember my father and you enjoyed your time." Placing her glass gingerly on the table, she takes care to dry her lips with a napkin, taking in her Grandfather's posture and face. "Many Lords and Princes still hunt and surely they would be quite fond of having their wife with them. Have my lessons with Lady Belle been truly satisfactory if my Lord or Prince is unhappy with my inability to understand the sport they so enjoy?"

Her Grandfather chuckles and finishes his glass off in a single gulp. "Sir Smith has certainly taught you well," he states with a smile, but then sighs. "Alice, my dear, you must understand by hesitation. You have been ill and you are all I have left in my bloodline."

"I fully understand but your hesitation is for naught. You and your many soldiers will be with me, should the hunt partake, so no threat would come to me."

Although Alice sees him slipping in her direction, he still holds firm to his conviction. "A hunt could take as much as a week, my dear, and you cannot fall farther behind in your studies. Making a Princess sleep outside and go long hours without rest or food – on the back of a horse nonetheless! – would surely shame my face to the public."

"Would it not gather more acceptable proposals?"

Instantly, her Grandfather's head jerks and stares at her with an odd combination of confusion and partial disgust.

"Would you dare marry a man who only takes to women who hunt?" he demands.

Chuckling, Alice replies with, "Of course not, Grandfather. What I insinuate is stronger alliances. An heir to the throne – a young girl, nonetheless – that can hunt without fear...what strength that could prove in the future!"

"How so?"

All the guards seem to be casting them curious glances but Alice ignores them and continues with her neat web.

"A Prince who hunts well can lead an army well," she tells him, seeing the spark of familiarity in her words. "A Princess who hunts without fear is a force to be reckoned with."

"Perhaps your father and I should have been more watchful of our talks," he mutters. "My decision stays the same Alice. I will not take you on a hunt."

Sighing, Alice does not break her straight posture when she says, "Very well, then. If that is your decision, I shall respect it."

This time he casts a searching glance towards her. Alice snatches a small roll of bread and eats it slowly and deliberately.

Alice can feel him searching her face and, when he sighs, she gives a small smile.

"With your argument before, I would be a fool to think you would give up so easily," he states, locking his eyes with hers once Alice lifts her head. "Why forfeit now?"

"To win a losing battle," she quotes, "you must pull back and draw from a different angle."

His eyes turn hard and his lips become tight, thin lines as he recognizes his own teachings.

"You are a fine King, Grandfather," Alice states, standing up, "and you have taught me much. I will not force you to take me on a hunt, as I am in no condition to be demanding things from you, but I will approach this from a different angle."

When the King stands, all the chatter amongst the guards cease.

"I forbid you to ever go on a hunt," he orders. "This is a command from your King and your guardian. Should you disobey your punishment will not be lessened."

Giving a single laugh, Alice stares down the King. Although she is much shorter in stature she feels far taller than he at their current time. To most punishments Alice has immunity.

"Grandfather, the only punishment you could possibly force upon me would be war," she reminds him. "Remember, I am the only heir to your throne, the last line of blood you have. Should you execute me or strip me of my title, who would be left? You would have to find another child to claim as your heir and, before that, assassinations would partake left and right. Do not forget the many enemies you have."

"Should an incident appear where punishments of exile or execution ever venture over your head, I will fulfill it as the King of this land. If you declare war on me, what of the allies I have? You have little according to your previous report."

"Number of allies is of little importance," Alice reminds him. "Strength and loyalty, though, is what determines the battle."

"Are you demanding war?"

Alice's sharp laughter cuts through the heavy silence in the room. "Grandfather, a fool would declare war while the enemy sleeps in their abode." Looking around the room, she smiles warmly. "You have caused an upstart with your guards, Grandfather. I mean neither war nor offense when I simply say that a hunt would be a good time to tour the kingdom, have fun, and simply bond over something nonpolitical for once." She pauses and looks around once more. "The last you have ever visited me on something unrelated to the kingdom was at the funeral of my parents. Getting to see you for something other than sadness or political reasons would be a change, would it not?"

Without saying anything more the King stalks out the room, two of the guards going with him and a maid leading him towards his room in a hurry. A few of the guards look at Alice, stunned by her words or maybe just stunned to know that a tiny Princess could possibly make their King act so rashly.

Regardless of their reasons Alice decides to retire herself, letting the guards know that they should not dally too long and that a maid will escort them to their rooms when ready. Once in her bedroom, exhausted from the day, she unfolds the piece of paper and smiles at the words.

It seems some things never change, Miss Alice.

Chapter 9

Alice jolts up in her bed, startled by whatever dream she cannot remember. Hugging herself as she attempts to calm her panicked heart, she looks around her room to make sure everything is in correct order. Lately she has been having nightmares that she cannot quite grasp and figures her kidnapping is slowly resting in her subconscious. Once Alice has calmed herself, she holds her head against a small headache and sighs heavily. As she gets less and less sleep her headaches grow. At least today's seems to be bearable, as the one a week ago had left her in bed the whole day.

Bringing back her curtains, Alice sees the sky still dark and sighs even heavier. Slipping on a coat and socks, Alice grabs her violin case and creeps outside of her manor, to the gardens under her favorite tree. Despite the chill, Alice deftly takes out her violin, tightens and rosins her bow before carefully perching the instrument on her shoulder.

Taking in a deep, icy breath, Alice closes her eyes and warms up with a few short songs before basking in a personal favorite, the melody of the song complex and quick, allowing her no chance to stop and think about the next note or placement, only allowing her mind to remember the beat.

Alice keeps her eyes closed even as she moves around in her garden, breathing short breaths and even starts to sweat despite the chill in the air.

As the song comes to a slow end, she opens her eyes, the sky lighting and her mind exhausted, she sighs with content just as the song finishes.

Clapping causes her to start and, when she turns to see the King, two of his guards, and much of her help standing at the door of her manor, Alice turns her head away, slightly embarrassed.

"I thought Lady Belle was exaggerating your skills," the King states. "It appears I underestimated you. You have certainly taken after your mother. Was it Vieuxtemps who wrote that?"

Although still stunned, Alice nods politely. "When did you...come out here?" she asks.

"I heard the sound of playing when I awoke and wandered out to find you," he says with a smile. "Your help came soon after I."

With rosy cheeks, Alice looks at all her help, smiling and seeming moved by her own work.

"Lady Belle exaggerates," Alice claims. "My skill is barely mediocre. My mistakes are those of beginners and my hands are clumsy."

"On the contrary, you sounded years more experienced than you are."

Snorting, Alice plucks a few strings to busy her chilling hands but says little else. Even though she knows that her help listen to her in the morning when she awakes, having them there is something else. Her cheeks are not red simply from the heat she built up.

"Dawn is swiftly approaching," the King observers, taking pity on his embarrassed granddaughter. "Breakfast shall be ready soon?"

Nodding, Alice turns to the chefs who quickly run away from sight and she sighs, sending a cloud floating towards the sky.

"Back to work," she orders. "The show is over. Get inside and get to work. We have many guests."

Quite a few chuckle but listen anyways, even though a few continue to dally by the door. When the King chuckles, Alice looks at him oddly.

"I will see you at the breakfast table," he says lightly and walks back in the house without another word.

Collapsing on the ground, placing the bow back in the case, Alice plucks a few more notes. Perhaps Anthony would have objected to her crash into music again, but she took it upon herself to discover why Chaos knows the music her mother used to play.

Back in the small fight Anthony and Chaos had, Alice was sure she was going to die so she was partially thrilled when she regained small control over her face and neck. She wanted to remember her mother's song, the one song she could only play twice without mistake no matter how many hours she studied the paper. She had hummed it in hopes to relive that memory but she had not expected the reaction.

When she saw Chaos start to writhe in further pain she simply continued the song unsure what would happen if the humming suddenly stopped. Alice could barely hear Anthony and Chaos talking, as though her humming had deafened her to anything except the sound of the melody. When she fell asleep in Anthony's arms she dreamed about her mother, of the paper with familiar notes and they were insisting her to play them. By the time Alice awoke she was aching to play on her violin but she could not play without *her* violin, the one that was broken years ago. Alice was surprised when the King sent her a violin and, for a reason Alice could not fathom, she fell in deep adoration of the antique, refusing to play on any instrument other than that one.

Alice's words to her Grandfather were true, but not on the same level as he thinks. Alice dreamed, for the days after she returned to her manor, of her mother playing, of the skill her mother held. Alice dreamed – whether it was truly a memory or a figment of her own imagination – of her mother's face as she played, of the faraway look and the fog that covered her mother's mind even after she stopped playing. To perform the piece of music her mother could play so deftly, Alice needed to improve her skills way beyond what they are.

As soon as Alice stands up, grabbing her bow during the rise, she starts to play again, needing with all her heart to improve. She tears through artists – Vivaldi, Mozart, Bach – without a second thought, taking their hardest songs in stride and playing them through her memory, unafraid to walk through the notes. Her fingers fly across the instruments neck, her bow sending rosin flying, hairs breaking under her pressure. Eventually, Alice falls to a slow, sad song, the notes seeming to cry out. Alice cannot seem to remember who wrote the song or what the name may be, but she plays the sorrowful song, letting herself get caught in the tide.

Miss Alice

By the time she stops playing to pack up her case, Alice's resolve has hardened. She mastered those songs when she was much younger, tackling the most difficult songs ever written without a second glance. She could – she *will* – play the song that made her mad captor writhe in pain, play the song her mother played masterfully and beautifully. If Anthony were to never return to her, she would have to be able to play the song for both defense and pride.

Alice's breath catches when she realizes that Anthony may not realize his error. She needs to meet the man who killed her family and find out for herself his action's reasons. She has made little headway in the seven years they have known each other, true, but surely she will find him. Once she becomes Queen things will most certainly become easier.

"Princess Alice?" calls a maid from the door, looking out with worried eyes. "Princess Alice, your breakfast is waiting and you Grandfather getting antsy."

Nodding, Alice stands with the case in her hand and walks towards her maid, who looks relieved to see Alice in front of her. She hurriedly leads Alice to the Dining Room where the guards are all fully armored, looking well rested – although a few quite pained – and much more observant. Her Grandfather has changed his robes and Alice realizes that she has not changed from her bed clothes.

"If you will excuse me for a brief more time," she says nicely. "Please, start eating without me. I will be back soon. Forgive me for my rudeness."

Before her Grandfather can give a gruff reply, she takes off down to her room. To her surprise, a deep purple dress lay on her bed, a pair of warm black socks on top and a purple ribbon for her hair. Smiling, she dresses quickly, runs a comb through her hair, ties a bow on the top of her head and grabs a pair of comfortable shoes. Once dressed, she examines herself in the mirror. Her dress is floor length and warm, her sleeves pooling around her wrists. Of course, the ribbon clashes with her pale hair, the dress her skin and eyes, making them appear brighter and paler then before. She looks childish and Alice smiles.

Hurrying out of her room, she comes to a halt outside her Dining Room and her knees buckle under her. She falls to the ground, grabbing the frame on her door to lag her descent.

Blood pools on the floor as all the guards lay slaughtered. Her Grandfather lay pinned against the wall, his eyes glazed over but his chest rising and falling faintly. Alice starts to tremble as she realizes another person stands in the room, his form soaked in blood but standing directly in the center.

She does not tremble in fear or terror, but from the sudden realization as to who the identity of her family's killer is. With the gap of time and her young, traumatized mind, perhaps it is not too surprising that she had not noticed the resemblance in the past but now the truth has been shoved in her face and everything seems to just disappear from her mind.

A surprised look on his face hurts Alice the most. He looks at her as though never expecting to see her here. He walks towards her but she backs up, crawling on her hands and knees, trying to reject the truth, not wanting to believe it.

He grabs Alice and holds her firmly but gently, and Alice finds herself unable to escape the revulsion and betrayal etching their way into her heart.

"Miss Alice, you were not supposed to come so soon," he whispers.

She turns a lashing glare to his familiar face. "How could you?" she asks softly, the hurt dripping off her voice so painful that he wishes she had yelled. "How could you betray me, Anthony?"

Chapter 10

"Tell me why you killed them, my prey, before I could collect their Cores."

Anthony sighs as he looks at Serene. "That would take far too long to explain," he says.

"I have the time," she replies back. "As do you. Now explain."

Anthony sighs and looks straight at her. "Telling you the explanation means that we need to go back to the beginning." He stares at Serene, holding her judging gaze carefully. "Back to when Chaos and I were first created."

Now, Serene's eyes narrow dangerously. "Why all the way back?"

"Because everything started then," Anthony replies. "You are well aware that all Demons are created when a human dies, but held enough malice or did enough wrong in their life to give them a second life."

Serene nods. "Depending on what the human did while they were alive will determine what the Demon is, and what they can do."

"Chaos and I were created roughly around the same time," Anthony tells her. "It was quite easy for us to grow in both intelligence and power. We started gaining more and more intelligence and tricked people quite easily into their contracts, gaining their Cores faster than others. We would take turns and, by the end of the human's squabbles, we would become the strongest Demons save the Demon King himself, although Chaos easily rivaled him.

"It is probably not a surprise when I tell you that soon after learning of this the Demon King practically gave him a job that kept him in line. Chaos did not see it as that, though, and continued to grow stronger. When he was officially appointed to his job, we had to split in our work efforts in order for me to keep growing. When I next saw him his power had immensely grown and I did not understand how it was possible. So, he decided to take me on a job with him.

"At first, the job was pretty simple. A family of five kids and a widowed mother. Two of the sons were off in the military, the third working on the farm to support everyone while the two younger girls had summoned us to them. We contracted instantly. Not long into the contract, the mother was murdered in front of Chaos's contracted girl's eyes and, when I met with her again, the power in her Core had grown tremendously. Chaos pointed out the one thing that every Demon knew but no one had ever taken advantage of. Can you guess what that was, Serene?"

To Anthony her face seems paler then before and her red eyes wide. Anthony waits for a long time, judging her reaction and waiting for her to reply. After a long silence, Anthony gives a single laugh.

"A human's Core is the base of all emotions," he reminds her. "The primary emotion that appeals to Demons is Anger, which can be stemmed off into two much more dangerous desires: the need for revenge and justice. Of course, the best way to create such forms of anger is for someone to experience a large wave of sadness, which is best stemmed from a death. Of course, having someone they know die in a horrible way is good, but letting them *see* it? That makes it even stronger and Chaos discovered this. When he told me, you could not imagine how ignorant I felt. It was a basic principle that everyone knew and yet everyone had let it so simply slip from their grasp."

Serene looks at him in disgust. "That is disgusting and wrong, Anthony. The reason no one has ever done it before is because it is wrong. Causing such sadness and anger in someone that you have made a contract with like that..." She glares at him. "That is not fair. It is a rule that you do not harm your contracted in any way. Not only would the emotional balance of your contracted be disturbed but the mental state would deteriorate."

Anthony sends her a sharp glance. "You are aware that it was *Chaos* who proposed that idea to the Demon King, correct? I am skipping ahead, I know, but I want you to be aware of that. Chaos wanted to make sure no other Demon would steal his idea after what happened."

Snorting, Serene twirls a red and platinum blonde streak together, swirling like the peppermint sticks that Alice eats during her winter holiday celebrations.

"Continue with your story, then," she grumbles.

"Well, Chaos and I slowly built up the torment around the two girls, even going so far as to widow the two girls." Anthony shrugs at Serene's glare. "When their children were old enough to work on their own, we fulfilled their contracts and took their Cores, leaving the girls' children in care of family friends. Of course, with such sudden power, it was bound to go wrong.

"Chaos has always been much more carefree about his actions than I, preferring to make a big show of things that require such little attention. One of the young boys caught sight of Chaos taking out the Core and sealing his mother's fate. Thinking nothing of it, I had decided to not tell Chaos of the boy's sighting.

"Many human years passed and we harvested Cores quicker than the first time, changing tactics numerous times. Eventually Chaos was called back and I decided to go scouting around. I was unaware of how many years had passed for the humans but I stumbled upon a Sanctuary where an older human man was talking with numerous others that had dubbed themselves as 'clerics.' They were planning on summoning the devil in the coming night and I had laughed at them."

Serene cracked a smile as well. "Humans that run Holy Sanctuaries are often the most popular to contract with," she states. "They call upon Demons faster than anyone could blink. Odd how humans believe them Holy, siphoning the words of God to them when they are really being told lies." She shakes her head. "Humans are certainly a gullible species."

Anthony nods in agreement. "That night I came out behind the church to watch, wondering who they would be summoning. Although they had said the 'devil,' I had to wonder who would appear. Would it be the Demon King himself, Chaos or another Demon all together? Of course, I should have seen the familiarity in the angry face of the older human man before this but, when Chaos was summoned, I heard the man's loud voice clearly and realized who the man was.

"They overpowered Chaos with such ease that I was stunned. I could not move while I watched them squirming on the ground or even when they placed a binding seal on his forehead. Of course when the older man carried him and walked inside of the barrier, I was further surprised. He dropped Chaos on the ground and the seal on his head began to glow brighter than anything I had seen in my life. Everything I had been taught and all that I had learned said that it was impossible for such seals to be possible for humans but, in a way, it made sense.

"Human anger can create Demons and creatures alike but, as I have said before, humans change with each new wave. This boy had prepared himself for this day and he bound his own body to the barrier, which is what causes Chaos to be stuck in his human form. He had left four kids of his own behind, you know, but he did it to seal his mother's murderer. All of this without the help of another Demon! Humans are curious beings."

Silence drapes the two as Anthony allows Serene to mull over what had been said. Anthony cannot understand why he sees disgust in her eyes, why she seems angry that he would do such things to get stronger. She had been with him in wanting to get stronger, to do anything to really become stronger, but now she seemed disgusted by it.

Miss Alice

Finally Serene sighs before saying, "There is more, I can assume."

Anthony smiles. "After Chaos was trapped, he let me in on another secret of his. Should something wrong be done in a single family, the Cores of each specific gender will become greater and greater as time goes on. So, because he did wrong to a female the first time and a male corrected the error, each time a female is born in that line the Core will become greater, while the males in the line will slowly gain power – first politically, then the power to do things humans cannot. This is why Chaos outlawed the growth in power for Cores, as he knew the dangers it could cause."

Sighing, Serene looks exhausted. "I cannot quite tell who the villain is in your fairy tale," she claims. "You make Chaos out to be dangerous and then make him seem in the light."

"Chaos is neither good nor evil," Anthony replies. "He strives for his own goal and will simply go to any side to reach it."

"Here I thought he was just insane," she grumbles. "Why are you so against him gaining more power if you obviously were such good friends with him at one point?"

"Quite simple. Once Chaos gains enough power, he will exterminate the human race as they will no longer be of any use to him, sealing him eternally as the strongest Demon. Would you truly want that?"

Serene's silence hangs over them and she simply looks away from him. "Get to the point," she snaps. "Why did you take my prey?"

"Truth be told, they were my prey to begin with," he says. "Chaos promised me the strongest Core of the family's line so I could rule with him. Even when I was with you, Serene, I watched over that family. But then you came upon them, a mere inconvenience at first. Of course, I knew they had a daughter but to ensure that the family line continued I needed them to have more than one child. I followed you when you were going to take the Core of Alice's dear mother and I was certainly surprised by what I found."

She snarls at him. "I was a fool to break such a rule," she snaps. "I was also a fool to take your downfall."

Chuckling, Anthony simply stares at her. "Serene, you were going to take two Cores at once – one from which you were not contracted with – and you were passing up such a wonderful opportunity. I led Alice to the brutal murder and I felt her Core's strength burst from the seams. Such power, Serene! Ah, but I had to play the waiting game, as the case was under investigation – for both the humans and the Demons – and a nice lapse of time would certainly be useful. Little did I anticipate the strength of Alice's Core when I would meet her again! Dear Serene, you were so helpful and yet so unaware."

"Were all the times we spent a web for your convenience?" she shrieks. "Was I simply a tool for you to use?!"

After a thoughtful moment, Anthony says, "At first, no. You were a wonderful ally, Serene, and you certainly helped pass the time and I contemplated telling you about the plan I had but then you found Alice's family."

"You let me be stripped of my position, be placed at the lowest ranking job any Demon could possibly have, because I found prey that you had not even claimed?" she demands. "That you now *illegally* claim?"

"You make it seem as though I forced you to take my downfall," Anthony states. "You did that on your own. We also agreed to say whoever we targeted as prey before we contracted with them. Honestly, the only person in the wrong here is you."

Anthony laughs when Serene's bony wings erupt from her back, the thin black material stretching raggedly over the bones, blocking out the sun. Every Harpy uses this as a threat, letting whoever they are showing their wings to that they are dangerous, but Anthony simply shakes his head with his smile still there.

"Your threat is of little meaning to me, Serene," he says. "I certainly hold more than enough power to overtake you."

"You have broken more rules then I care to count," she mutters, folding her wings back into her back. "What stops you from simply barging into a barrier?"

"Simply that I cannot without permission," he says. "I am contracted, remember?"

"That I wish I understood," she remarks. "You are contracted to the human you have slaughtered countless in her family. Do you not think you are taking quite a risk?"

"Perhaps if Alice ever discovered the truth but the chances of that happening are slim to none – even if Chaos mentions things he should not, I can smooth it over." Anthony shrugs. "In time, once her Core has reached its potential, I will inform her and take her Core then."

"Do you know no shame?" she asks. Anthony does not get a chance to reply to her strange question. "I have never met the girl nor do I ever plan to but I have heard from multiple sources of the failed contracting attempts with her. Three years of Demons chasing her and she never broke her glare to say no. She rejected you *twice* and then placed her life within your hands and you treat her as such!" Shaking her head, Serene presses her hand against the invisible wall before it breaks open in a large gap, forming an entrance the width and height of Anthony.

Anthony looks at her in surprise. His surprise grows when Serene's glare intensifies. Anthony has to look away from her.

"I pity the poor human who will eventually learn this truth," she says. "I pity you, Anthony, as you were such a kind man once. More so, I pity that I will not see your contracted beat you when she learns the truth."

Now, Anthony's eyes turn to blood red slits. "What do you mean?"

"If what I have heard of Alice to be true," she states, "then I would pity any man – human, Demon, animal, perhaps even plant – that would dare cross and betray her."

"How would you know anything of Alice?" he demands.

"A many men and Demons tell tales to me of the formidable human who is a joy to be allied with, but a terrifying adversary when crossed or angered. I believe the name Alice appeared more than once." She sighs and points to the door. "Go and rescue your damsel, Anthony. Be her knight for now and later be the dagger that stabs her in the back. Go and reap the rewards that you have sown."

After a few steps Anthony hears Serene say, "Although I have to wonder, will the reaped be as sweet as the sown?"

Ignoring the girl, Anthony left, her words perhaps leaving a larger affect than he knew then.

Chapter 11

In the present as Alice glares at him, her eyes lashing like whips but churning like waves. Anthony sees her mind working behind those eyes, sees the hurt in her face. He had picked the purple dress as it would be harder to visibly stain something darker when she would appear in the lurid scene. Anthony had predicted the time to dress and to ready herself would take longer so he could get away from the scene beforehand. He had not planned for this.

"Miss Alice, let me explain," he starts but is cut off by the angered girl.

"What could you possibly do to ameliorate this?" she demands. "You have lied to me this whole time. What more do you need from me? Take my Core, Anthony, as I need no explanation from you as to why you would kill my family."

"Miss Alice I believe you are being irrational," he states, grabbing her wrist to keep her from fleeing.

Alice does not give him a second's extra to gather the next word, choosing instead to thrash in Anthony's grip until he has to release her or risk Alice injuring herself. Although her legs give out, Anthony makes no attempt to reach for her, knowing what little good it would do and waits for her to stand.

"Why do you wait?" she demands. "Why do you talk instead of gaining what is yours? These past seven years – they have been *nothing* to you. You watched me run around for seven years while hiding the truth away." She takes a piece of the fabric and tears it down, leaving the cotton layer exposed as the purple silk falls to the sides. She yanks his hand and presses it against the bottom of her chest. "Take it! What is there to stop you?"

Anthony can feel the Core pulsing against her chest, the anger and hurt thrumming wildly and he can even feel the other emotions rampaging within said emotions...but he restrains himself. Gritting his teeth, he pushes her away a few steps. Composing himself in a few seconds Anthony stares at her easily.

"Miss Alice, the deal we made was for you to find the man who murdered your family and understand his reasoning for it," he states. "As long as the latter part is unfulfilled, I cannot obtain your Core."

"What explanation could a Demon give me that would not lead to cold blood?" she snarls. "You have been selfish in the time we have spent together. I am only yours, as I am the key to your success, being the main source. Your reason for killing my parents seems clear to me. You want my Core so badly you fell inside of your greed."

When Alice sees Anthony's expression turn from the calm composure to utter surprise she knows she has hit the truth and she smiles smugly despite the situation.

"Perhaps my greed had something to do with it," Anthony admits, "but the whole truth is much more complex than a simple word. Miss Alice, if you would listen to what I must say then—"

All the wind flies from Anthony's lungs as he watches his strong contractor just crumble at his words. Alice crumples back down to the ground and her body begins to tremble. At first he thinks she is simply angry but something else catches his attention. Her feeling of anger has dropped dramatically and he cannot pick out the emotion she has. He watches as she buries her face in her hands and hears her take sharp breaths for a few moments before moving her hands away to glare at him. He is taken aback by her red face, at her eyes watering so profusely.

Then he recognizes the sound as he had heard it once before. He had been outside her room, only weeks ago. That uncharacteristic sound he had heard now displayed so vividly on her face.

"My embarrassment for ever crying in front of you is nothing compared to how angry I am," she chokes. "You have lied to me, Anthony. You have murdered my family and have belittled me to a simple child again. My words may be wasted on you – as my Core is much more valuable than my petty anger, I would imagine – but you know me well and perhaps my words will make some small dent in your mind. I truly am ashamed of what you have done."

"Miss Alice—"

"I am not *finished*." She roughly brushes her hand across her face. "I may be unable to harm you in any way but if in these seven years you learned anything about me, then you should feel something at this: I truly did trust you more than myself and perhaps in my naiveté I believed you a friend. Now...now I see you on the same level as the foolish Lords who came to my door asking for ridiculous things, thinking me a child." She shakes her head. "I thought you would be better than them, Anthony. Perhaps there is no life form out there that can—"

Her voice breaks off and she turns her face away. Anthony reaches towards her, wanting to give some amount of comfort but his hands are slapped away and, with a strange glare, Alice runs off.

Serene's final words echo in his head and he turns around to punch the wall, leaving a large hole there. Years and years of being the composer, trampled by a mere human playing in the background. Everything he had planned and played. Each deck he renewed and every cheat he pulled, suddenly done away with.

No way could he mend this fracture. No way could he smooth it over and no way would Alice let him near her now. Perhaps before, when she claimed he lied to her and broken a promise but now that mending dream has splintered into tiny shards.

Pressing his head against the wall Anthony grits his teeth, trying to think of how he could have gone wrong. Everything had been played perfectly, each movement predicted. Perhaps the mistakes were too small for him to see or perhaps too near. As

Anthony sifts through the past, trying to find the source of the splinter, he fears he will never find what he seeks.

With a flash of blinding intensity, Anthony jerks up his head and looks towards the area where Alice ran off to. He shakes his head and slams his palms against the wall, causing it to shudder.

Of course she would remember that promise, made when they had barely begun making their contract. He had taken Alice home and set her to bed and, while he was working in the silent house, Alice found him straightening up the kitchen. She had a stubborn look on her face but something like fear clung to her. Anthony was surprised, as he had never scented the emotion on her, not even when the Demons had attacked her in the cemetery.

"Anthony?" she asked, her voice quiet in the silent house. "Those Demons are not going to come back, right? You said they were never coming back."

Nodding, Anthony smiled at her. "Others will come, perhaps, but not those three."

She nodded and the stubbornness in her face grew greatly and the scent of fear dwindled.

"I wanted to be sure," she told him. "I do not wish to be caught off guard again."

"If I am with you, Miss Alice, I doubt you will ever be caught off guard again, although it is not something I could promise," he told her. She nodded and started to walk away. When she got to the door, Anthony said, "Although I can promise that you will never feel fear again."

Right then Alice stopped at the door and, without turning around, she said, "I am never afraid so it will be an easy promise to keep."

For whatever reason Alice kept that promise in her head and, during the time she spent with Chaos, perhaps she felt fear again. He was hardly to blame for breaking a promise he never knew had been broken – or had even thought could be broken. She had certainly never let on that she had been afraid. He could hardly be blamed for such a thing. Yet had Alice not also been angry at any promise broken? She has scolded kids in town when she heard them bickering about broken promises and had even broken a trade agreement with territory from the far north because he had promised to never increase the price or decrease the amount of goods. It should be no surprise to him that Alice would be mad over this promise when others had been of greater or lesser value and her anger had been worse.

Finally, her words start sinking in. He did understand Alice, knew her personality and her standards. For some reason he did feel ashamed of himself for letting her down. He felt foolish for trying doing the things he had done, for crossing Alice, but for reasons he could not fathom. He has spent decades with others and had never once felt this demeaned when the truth was exposed. He has seen countless others cry as a result of his words and actions, countless others claim to be ashamed of him. Their words were meaningless to him.

In seven years a simple yet complex human had affected him greater than decades of helping Kings tear down civilizations and lead them to victory in war. Alice was the only human who had dared yell at him and hold his glare. Who required him to do and say things at a certain time while acting and speaking in a completely different manner. She had treated him as she had everyone else and yet that had never annoyed him like it had from others before.

Turning away from the hole in the wall, he looks into the room and calls for assistance and many of the help do come. Their faces pale in confusion and turn to Anthony for explanations.

"Mister Anthony, what happened?" asks a frantic maid. She looks back at the mess in the room. "Was it the same man as before? Did he break in again? Oh...how is Princess Alice?"

"It does appear to be the same man," Anthony says. "Why was there no one to watch over him? Did I not tell the guards here to watch the King just as strictly as the Princess?"

"Th-they must have changed shifts," the maid replies, flustered. "Should the police be informed?"

"Do as you see fit," Anthony replies. "I have some matters to attend to. Make sure the Princess does not see this again."

Before the maid can say much else, Anthony is walking away and many others come in to assist. They clean the King and place him in a guest room, clean the slaughtered guards and cover their faces with thin blankets. When the room is cleaned they close it off for appearance and not even a whisper is spoken between the help while they attempt to clean the mess that Anthony has made.

Moving into his study Anthony collapses in his chair and stares at the ceiling. He smiles grimly as he looks down at his bloodied clothes. He starts to wonder about Alice, at what makes her so special. Perhaps he should have taken her Core at the given chance or even gone after her, but he had done nothing. He wonders what had stopped him, what compelled him to watch her run away. He tries to find reason behind it but the root seems to evade him.

Perhaps in my naiveté, I believed you a friend. A friend? To Alice? Absurd. Alice did not have friends, as no child could keep up with her and no adult enjoyed her company for long. To think Alice would even consider him a friend, someone who would eventually steal her ability to fully be a human, baffles him. Perhaps her grief clouded her judgment and she chose the wrong words.

"Princess Alice Millersky," he says to the empty room. "The most peculiar and complex human alive, and just perhaps the most difficult to let go of."

Chapter 12

Alice sits in her garden, behind the giant tree that once held the four baby birds. She hugs her knees close to her, the purple silk of her dress slowly being ruined by the wetness of the ground, of the dirt, but Alice does not care. Her heart screams out, angry and betrayed, but so sad.

Why am I so sad? Alice asks. *What makes my chest ache so harshly? What makes my tears fall without my control?*

She has known since the beginning of her contract that Anthony would eventually steal her Core and she had accepted it long ago. She saw the resistance, the hesitation when she had put his hand on her chest. He wanted it but what held him back? He claims that their contract has yet to be fulfilled but it has. She understands his motives and no story must be said in order for the picture to be complete.

Perhaps it should not surprise me, Alice thinks. *He has broken his promises before.*

Only in the beginning, when he was unaware of Alice's temper, her expectations of him. He would say it was for her best interest for him to go against his words but she still did not like it. "I promise you I will not say this," or "I promise you I will not do that." Simple promises that he would break and she had lashed out to him, punishing him as she saw fit. When he learned of her expectations, of her holding his word, he started abiding her rules, even if they were bent slightly. She did not mind although she did always try to find a way to complain to him. As always, though, he kept to his word. He forgot his promise, made a long time ago, but was it because he truly forgot due to the promise being so easy to uphold, or because he tried to hurt her?

Anthony would not hurt me intentionally, she thinks. *No, I carry what he desires.*

All those times he told her over and over again. "I will not hurt you, Miss Alice." Just words truly and perhaps they were smoke and mirrors but she has believed them. She had believed he would protect her when she could not protect herself. She placed herself in his hands when Chaos kidnapped her. She had believed in him and yet her anger clouded those thoughts. She had seen him more than an ally, more than simply a tool as so many others are to her.

A friend, though? Alice wonders. *Did my childish mind want me to believe I had a friend, for once in my life, as my fate is undoubtedly sealed?*

Nothing she said to him made sense as she reflects back on it. Perhaps feeling ashamed in him was correct, as she did want him to be shamed and the knowledge of his betrayal stung her deeply, but little else seemed right in her mind. He had only said "you are only mine" a handful of times, after all, and who is she to judge on being greedy when she has never given to a charity or helped a starving child?

Alice lifts her head towards the clear sky and thinks. The King did not look well and she had no other family that could care for her. She would have to take the throne should the King not recover and thus she would have to marry to continue the bloodline of her family. Would she even make it to her Grandfather's funeral? It seems unlikely with these events. She would take control of her kingdom, be responsible for so much more, become the greatest Queen the land has ever known – now, it could all be wistful dreams.

What a drastic turn my life has taken, Alice thinks. *Why am I so sad? This is the path I took knowing my fate and where I would end up but why does it make me so sad now?*

115

Standing up, Alice moves around in the garden to where she can see into the study. She sees him and, although she tries to hate him, to turn the sadness in her chest to anger, it only makes her sadder. He looks confused, puzzled by whatever thought is running through his head. Turning away from him, she closes her eyes tightly and walks towards the edge of her manor's territory, right outside the walls and close to the forest. Everything is quiet here and Alice feels herself calm down.

She finds a spot under a dormant tree and surrounded by shrubbery where she just lies down and curls herself into a ball. Alice does not care that her pale blonde hair will be a mess of dirt and twigs tomorrow or that her purple dress is now beyond repair. She does not care that the chill could easily turn her from pale to stone cold – and just as unmoving. Alice wants to curl into a ball, close her eyes and wake up from the nightmare she is surely having.

My childish mind decides now, of all times, to flame alive again, Alice thinks as she drifts off. *Or perhaps my childish mind never died to begin with.*

As soon as Alice falls asleep, Anthony hears the sound he hoped to never hear again: screeching metal and he smells something worse than before. A creature he has never heard before screams as it is released.

He stands and rushes out, searching every room and all the gardens for Alice but finding no sign. Thunder rumbles through the manor and light from the lightning dance in the sky. A beautiful sight if not for the sounds that ride with the storm.

Many of the help are running around, confused and unsure of what to do.

"Mister Anthony!" hails one, a younger boy. He runs up, eyes darting around. "Mister Anthony, have you seen Princess Alice? We have not seen her since this morning." He looks pityingly at Anthony. "I heard you two had a fight again, sir."

Cursing under his breath, Anthony says, "It is your job to keep up with her. I have seen nothing of her since she left my sights." He looks outside. "Stay indoors and search the manor. We will find her."

Anthony starts to walk towards the door but is stopped by the boy's call. "But, Mister Anthony, where are you going? To search outside? Is that safe with this storm?"

Anthony does not bother to look back at the boy when he says softly, "To find an old friend."

Although the boy wants to object, he holds his tongue and watches as Anthony walks out the door. Before he hurries off, the boy scratches his head in confusion and says, "Geez, what does Alice see in that Demon?" Waiting another few seconds, he shrugs and hurries to complete his given task.

When Anthony steps outside, he does a brief search for Alice and just barely catches her scent. He nods in the direction of where she is and hurriedly moves forwards. Thunder and lightning explode around Anthony, shaking the ground. Looking up, Anthony's eyes go very wide as he sees the sky.

Back in the house, the boy quickly passes Anthony's message to others in the house. He hears thunder boom, enough to shake the walls of the manor and he peeks outside and gives a dark smile. The boy looks back to the hurrying help, all calling for their Princess. He walks around before coming to a shaded corner. He leans back and sighs. Looking towards the window again, he hears the crackle and braces the candle stand as the walls shake and lightning flashes outside in the clear, cloudless sky.

"Hey, kid!" calls a maid, a panicked look on her face. The boy sits up from his spot to meet the maid. "Who are you? No, there isn't time for that. Have you seen the Princess?"

"If you wait by the doors to the garden, you will see her," the boy says. "At least, that is where I last saw her."

"Thank you!" the maid says and then pauses, looking at the boy's eyes. "You have..." Shaking her head, she looks at the boy's eyes again and sees them as blue. "I guess it was a trick of the light.

I thought your eyes changed colors. My worry must be clouding my head. Thank you again!" With that, she hurries off to the garden door.

Smiling, the boy leans backwards and disappears into the shadows.

Chapter 13

When Alice awakens the sky has darkened and people are calling her name urgently and worriedly. As Alice becomes fully aware she sees the dirt and frowns before remembering, which makes her grimace. Holding her head up high, she stands up and walks from the cover of the forests. Alice hears the thunder and the crackle of lightning and thinks little of it.

Just before Alice reaches the full view of her house she snaps her head up and looks at the sky. A dark blue cloudless sky, and even though not fully lit, the moon is starting to shine. A crackle of lightning erupts over her head and her skin prickles from the sparks coming from nowhere.

Alice moves into sight of the house and a maid runs out, relief on her face.

"Princess Alice!" she says, relief visible on her face. "Hurry, Mister Anthony needs everyone—"

Before she can complete the sentence she falls to the ground. Turning around slowly Alice barely has time to understand the face she sees when a hand yanks her back out of sight from the house and another covers her mouth. She bites down on the hand but the owner of the hand does not seem to notice. They drag her back into the woods and then she sees an even more familiar face.

"Hello, Alice," Chaos says, sitting down as the two men push her to the ground. "I assume you are pleased with my choice of servants? They do appear more human than my gargoyles."

Looking back at them Alice sees the familiar faces but she is confused. She sees the gray hair, the black stripe on the top, his weathered face and harsh brown eyes but does not comprehend it. Alice knows the boyish face, the brown hair and tanned skin and certainly recognizes the gaping hole in his chest but his eyes are devoid of anything now.

"I do not understand," she says. "What is Rowan doing here? He is dead. The dead do not come back to life; it is impossible."

"Anything is possible," Chaos replies, "with the correct resources. Lord Edgar surprised me, as you called him dimwitted but you certainly appear to fit the title more. Rowan is as alive as he will ever be. He is being held here by a Fate Weaver, you see. These beautiful creatures collect souls and then play marionette – at my bidding, of course. In reality he is barely here at all."

"Why are you here?" she demands. "Why are any of you here?"

Chaos flashes Alice a grin before holding her chin between his finger and thumb. "Dear Alice, I have yet to claim what is rightfully mine. Why would I not come back to claim my treasure?"

"Stop toying with her, Chaos!" snaps Edgar. He points the gun at Alice's head and smiles. "You murdered my son when everything I had planned would have benefitted you and my family. I was planning on giving you a kind and graceful death Alice but now my only wish is for you to die!"

A shot goes off and the bullet is stopped mere centimeters from the gun. Chaos turns a threatening smile towards Edgar, who recoils slightly.

"To die ignorant is the worst death," Chaos says calmly. "Let me speak with her."

Grumbling, Edgar backs down and he stares at Rowan who stares at Alice unblinkingly.

Chaos crosses his legs and smiles kindly at Alice. He reminds her of a little boy and she could almost forget that he could be vile and threatening when angry. Alice keeps her memories of him strongly in her mind, reminding herself not to let her guard down around this Demon.

"Now, Alice," Chaos states. "You really are an ignorant little human. Had our time together been little more than a bump in the road? Well nonetheless I am here now thanks to you."

Blinking, Alice says, "What do you mean? I do not remember ever summoning people such as yourself nor Edgar and his decaying son to my land."

"But Alice, you set the stage," he says grandly, spreading his arms out. "You birthed the anger in Edgar's chest by killing his son, you escaped my clutches in the barrier and then you did not even play the song that had kept me locked away for so long. Dear Alice you truly begged me to come and find you."

"I do not understand what you are saying," she says. "What song do you mean? You were never trapped behind the barrier, either. You, like the creatures you summoned, were free to leave, were you not?"

Blinking for a moment, Chaos breaks into a laugh that sends him falling backwards. He laughs loudly and fully before looking at Alice's face.

"You truly do not know," he says, laughing for a moment again. "How bittersweet, Alice! That foolish Anthony has still told you nothing? Left you as ignorant as a mere baby! How bittersweet, Alice." Chaos motions for the two men behind him to sit down and after a moment they both comply. Alice almost gags as the scent of decay floats over to her but she gets a glare from Edgar and a grin from Chaos, causing her to keep herself together. "That song you hummed when we last saw each other – that song held the barrier, in which I was a prisoner in, together. It kept the seal that your great-great-great-great-great-great-great-Grandfather placed on me when he sealed me in there."

"I have not played the violin in years," she reminds him. "You cannot be correct."

121

Chaos sighs and holds his head. "Alice, meek-minded logic gets you nowhere in any world. Your many-times-over-great-Grandfather put the seal with a failsafe to ensure someone plays the song: should the correct song not be played then the generation which should be playing it will be the number of years it takes to fall. You are the tenth generation so you had ten years. As you could not play it accurately the two times you did manage to play it, the barrier continued to weaken." He smiles. "Now, here I am. In the flesh, seeing you. Sadly the seal that bound me to my human form is unable to be broken. Your many-times-great-Grandfather is such a pain."

Alice stares at him, confused and unbelieving.

"Humans have two phrases that I have always enjoyed," Chaos tells her, leaning forwards as his eyes sparkle like little children's at Christmas. "One of which I have already mentioned. The other would be 'knowledge is power' as it is so correct. The more you know about someone, the more you can hurt them, the more you can tear them down. Is that not exciting, Alice? Is that not why you have always drowned yourself in studies when you lose someone or felt sad?" Chaos's eyes sparkle brightly as he sees Alice tense. "Perhaps not only sadness though. Fear, maybe?" He catches her glare and laughs. "Oh, certainly, I caught your nerve, did I not?"

Alice glares at him but tries to think. He has gained knowledge of her. Did she not tell him to research her, though? Alice stems through everything about herself as he stares at her, smiling and laughing. *Can he read minds?* Alice wonders before shaking it away. It would have surely shown long before now if he could.

"You are such an interesting human, Alice," Chaos states. "You are not easily tracked nor do you leave trails around you. Rabbit trails, perhaps, but never direct trails. I wonder Alice, is it because of your personality or your status? Do people respect you because of you or because of the crown you will inherit?"

"I would be a fool to believe that people only respect me for me," she tells him. "Of course many – if not all – would respect me solely for my crown. But just as many will try to use me and think me a fool." She sends the last comment towards Edgar, who glares right back at her and makes a point of slowly reloading his gun, although she doubts many bullets were misplaced.

Chaos laughs, as though watching the two is unquestionably the funniest thing in the world. He observes Alice as she examines the young human male, who stares at her with empty eyes. Chaos wonders how long the Fate Weavers can keep the badly injured body. They had done many repairs on the body before this but it is still in a horrible state. Chaos cannot help but want to stay longer with Alice, to see her unravel. She is so close; he could almost smell her instability today.

Then, he stops and looks around, curious.

"Edgar," Chaos says. "Did you not fire a bullet at the maid?"

Blinking, Edgar replies with, "Yes, I did."

"Did you not fire it close to the house? And guns do make a loud bang, correct?"

"Yes, for both," Edgar tells him. "Why do you ask?"

"Perhaps I am the *only* one with a brain around here," Chaos says in a bored voice, "but should Anthony not have heard the gun? With Alice missing one would think he would come running as soon as he heard the bang and smelled the blood of the maid."

Alice makes a face that Chaos notices and he leans forwards to look at it. He has not seen this look on her face before, so his curiosity explodes.

"What is that face for, Alice?" he asks. He sees the deep frown on her face and would guess some kind of sadness but there was very little anger. Instantly he tenses and grabs her shoulders. "Alice, what is it? What happened?"

Pushing him away, Alice sends a much weaker glare than what Chaos has come expect from her.

"Anthony and I had an... argument, if you want," she says. She sharply glares at him and raises her voice to make a crisp, cold tone. "What is it to you, though?"

When Chaos frowns he feels both Edgar and Alice stiffen but ignores them. He looks at Alice's chest, sensing her glowing Core, feels its intensity, but it feels...tainted. Anger makes it stronger and it is certainly strong – any Demon could tell you that – but he had never felt sadness in a Core so deeply etched as this. *If this argument was enough to produce such sadness,* Chaos thinks while watching Alice, *Anthony should have taken her Core then and there. Humans do tend to overreact to insignificant things and Alice certainly can make a show of her emotions.* Chaos can feel her sadness pouring from her Core and tries to think it through but to little avail. *What could possibly cause Alice such intense sadness?*

"What has he said to make you so sad?" Chaos asks, his eyes scrutinizing her face, waiting for some sign to give a hint at what may have happened. Instantly Alice closes her face off and puts on her stubborn front: head raised, sitting straight, glare poised in her eyes, and no stray hair blemishing her face. Before she even speaks, Chaos believes he knows her answer.

"I am not sad," she snaps. "Irritated is more like it. Irritated that you would dare kidnap me for a second time and bring this brute and his decaying son to my manor."

Edgar's mouth opens to say something but Chaos holds up his hand to silence him. "She has a right to be irritated with the last bit," he simply states. "I certainly get mad when someone brutish pops by and brings his decaying son as well."

"He is not *decaying*," Edgar snaps. "The Weavers prevent the body from decaying."

"Well, that would take far too long to explain," Chaos says lazily. "If what Alice says is true, that she and Anthony had a...falling out...then I guess there is little point in keeping the theatrics to a low." Chaos gives a mischievous grin towards Edgar who looks slightly perplexed. "Alice, you can choose to believe me or not but I believe you should know that everything you thought you knew about your dear friend Anthony was all a lie." He leans in close, as though telling her a secret, and Alice leans backwards, trying to keep her distance from the strange man. "A lie in order to grow your Core to extreme power and overtake *me*." His eyes sparkle and Alice wonders, for the briefest heartbeat, if this peculiar man has always been so eccentric, if his eyes had been anything else other than black pools. "After all, should he overtake me, he will have more than enough power to control all the Demons. Would that not be tasteful?"

Before Alice can get a word out, another bullet is fired and Chaos does not stop it. Alice gasps in pain, her gray eyes widening and she leans over, holding her shoulder and trying to fight back the fiery pain spreading down her arm. She looks over at Edgar, clenching her jaw to prevent a single sound from escaping, and sees him smiling madly.

"No killing," Chaos says in a sing-song voice. "I need her Core after all. Have your fun, human Lord, but do not kill her."

Alice does not completely comprehend his words, too wrapped up in her strange wound. She has been fired at before but she never had to worry about being hit. All her life, protected by someone – some willing to let themselves die while others know no such fear. Perhaps, should she have realized her immediate threat, she could have done something. Rolled away, ducked? Anything if she had thought it would make the bullet miss.

"Rowan, dear boy, restrain her," Edgar orders, gesturing towards Alice with his gun. For a moment, Rowan does not react but, eventually, he lumbers over and hooks his arms through Alice's. Alice nearly gags – both from pain and from the stench of Rowan's decaying body. Chaos laughs and Alice closes her eyes, refusing to let her eyes fill or to let the vile men see the pain coursing through her body.

"Stand her up," Edgar says. Chaos says something cheerfully in reply but his words are lost to Alice. As Rowan pulls her up, yanking on her injured shoulder, she screams out, unable to help herself. Her vision tunnels for a moment but she regains some control of herself but not in time to stop the tears.

"Perhaps the other shoulder now," Edgar says, his voice light but thoughtful, as though discussing which crops he wants to have planted. "What say you, Chaos?"

A small lapse of silence before he says, "Perhaps that would be the best place, considering anything else has major arteries. Having her bleed out, although as fun as it is, certainly would be against better preferences." He sends a smile towards Alice, who musters all her strength to glare at him. "We would not want to waste your Core, would we Alice?"

Looking up, Alice sees Edgar take aim and, before he can fire, she looks at him and says, in the most breathless and frail voice she has ever used in her life, "Such a shame that you would use your rage like this, Edgar. You are much more...dimwitted than before."

He aims and fires, this time grazing her side. She screams until her throat hurts but all she hears in reply is the laughter of the two men. Rowan's grip on Alice does not lighten up and Alice knows, without a doubt, that she has no way of escaping this time. She had always thought that, even once Anthony had taken her Core and left, that she would be protected from any harm. By then she would have someone to rule beside her, perhaps and heir of her own, but to think it would end this way....

She gives a painful exhale that was initially a laugh. Chaos glances at her oddly.

"What do you find humorous, Alice?" Chaos asks.

Alice shakes her head, unable to muster enough strength to lift it up. Another pain filled exhale escapes her and something almost like a smile coats her lips, but only for a heartbeat. Alice cannot tell what hurts her worse anymore but she does not care. After all, Chaos was right: Anthony would have heard the gunshot earlier, smelled the blood of the maid. Even now he would have heard her scream and smelled her blood so why, *why* did he not come? Obviously because he has no use for her...right? She had discovered his lies after all, so what use did she really have left? If he truly wanted her Core, he would have taken it then and there. Perhaps it is no use to him anymore.

"Perhaps I should retrieve her Core," Chaos muses. He walks over and grabs her chin, causing her to cringe from the pull on her shoulder. "She looks awfully pale."

Edgar snorts, lowering his gun slightly. "Do what you think is best," he says gruffly. "I just want her dead by the end of this."

Chaos chuckles a bit, shaking his head as though finding Edgar humorous. He lifts his other hand and Alice wonders if she will even feel that pain. She cannot imagine any pain more than that of bullets in her body.

Closing her eyes, Alice slumps even more against Rowan's hold, cringing against her shoulder and feels her tears fall off her cheeks.

"Oh Rowan," Alice hears Edgar say. He sounds very far away to her ears. "Why not help Chaos? Keep her propped up. One arm around her stomach – yes, like that – and one against her shoulders. Perfect." Alice stifles a cry, allowing a loud whimper to escape her lips. Her wounds throb with intensified pain and she feels Chaos's hand on her chest.

"Any last words, Alice?" he asks, genuine kindness in his voice.

She considers it for a moment. Alice does not think she could honestly speak but she does think her last words.

How foolish we humans are, she thinks to herself, staring at the black pools of Chaos's eyes. *We ask for help from these creatures yet...not much help is given in return. A petty wish, a desire for something so strong we would banish all else away! How foolish.*

Turning her head away in one last act of defiance, she looks around one more time. To die in a place where she always found solace – out in nature under large canopying trees – is not horrible. Alice thinks back to what she had asked, so long ago, of Anthony. How many times had he saved her? How many times had he corrected her and argued with her? Alice thinks of her teachers: Sir Smith and Lady Belle. All those times Alice had argued and fought them yet they came back. The town pastry baker, always greeted Alice with a smile, ignoring the crown that would eventually sit on her head, seeing only the young girl. The King, dead and with no heir to continue on his line. The kingdom, which would surely fall now that their royals had fallen.

All gone from the small act of walking into a room too early.

Closing her eyes, Alice keeps the image of all the people still alive, wondering if they will miss her. In her mind, Alice scoffs at the idea. People missing her? Impossible, as she never gave them a reason to want to miss her. Still, the question lingers longer then Alice would like it to.

"Well," Chaos says, quiet and seeming very far away, "I guess this is goodbye, Alice. I thank you for your help." Alice can hear the smile in his voice, although his voice grows ever fainter to her ears. "Perhaps, Alice, I will see you in Hell."

Alice feels searing pain, than she falls to the ground. Alice grabs for unconsciousness, happily succumbing to dark numbness, before the pain settles fully into her body.

Chapter 14

Silence coated in shock seeps through the air surrounding the two befuddled men. Edgar looks at his son, incomprehension plain on his face while Chaos looks at the three unseen Fate Weavers above his head, madly spinning in circles. He had seen the strings cut but had thought it was simply their inability to hold onto the body anymore.

"Rowan!" Edgar yells. "What are you doing, son? Hold up Alice!"

Chaos looks down at the unconscious girl and then looks at the Weavers. Barely three strings stay on his skin, the ones that hold the boy's life together. Chaos had assumed he was long gone but perhaps his conscious is still there within those strings.

Edgar continues to yell and scream at his son but Chaos watches Rowan silently. He sees the slight twitch of a muscle and Chaos cannot believe it. He laughs coldly and stares at the boy, some focus in his glass eyes. In a single, lightning-fast movement, Rowan's decapitated body falls to the ground. Edgar stares in horror and betrayal towards Chaos who shakes his hand to get the disgusting liquids off.

"What was that for?" demands Edgar.

Holding the Weavers close to him, Chaos says, "Did your son not have an… infatuation for Alice?"

For a moment Edgar seems unable to respond. "Yes, he did," Edgar finally admits. "What does that have to do with you decapitating my son?"

"That was little more than a puppet using the shell of the boy," Chaos snaps. "That *thing* no longer had a will to live, Edgar. Stop pretending your son was ever alive after his heart was devoured." Taking a deep breath, Chaos releases the Weavers before turning to look at Edgar. "Your son's mind was still intact, which means all his memories and ability to remember emotions lasted. Although his Core is far away, he remembered that infatuation for Alice and managed, for a flicker of a second, to regain control over his body and release Alice."

"But I thought—"

"Humans are despicable creatures," spits Chaos. "They do not understand when to give up. It is pathetic."

"Perhaps so, but it is also what makes them such a strong race."

Chaos and Edgar snap their heads to the trees. Anthony sits on a tree limb, high up and out of sight from them. His face is not angry nor is his gait threatening as he walks towards Chaos after jumping from the tree. Chaos sees him glance towards the sky and Chaos tries to follow Anthony's line of sight but only sees a large bird disappear after a few heartbeats. He does not even glance at Alice, who looks worse than before.

"What are you doing here?" Anthony asks, curiosity in his voice. "Last time we met I asked you to schedule a visit." Anthony looks briefly at the decapitated young boy and Edgar, who has his gun trained on Anthony's head as though expecting it to do anything. "I certainly did not expect you to ever stoop so low as to partner with the likes of Chaos. I thought you had more common sense."

Both men are disturbed by Anthony's calm voice. Nothing about him registers to them as threatening: not his stance, his words, how he holds each man's eyes for a few seconds before darting to the next, absolutely nothing gives them reason to be concerned. Chaos is curious as to why. His contracted is on the ground, bleeding and wounded, and he waited until now to show himself? For what purpose? If he had been here any time before this, why let his contracted receive that kind of pain before stepping in?

"I came here to claim what belongs to me," Chaos replies guardedly. "Alice informed me you two had a...falling out, her words not mine. What was it about?"

Anthony shrugs leisurely. "I slaughtered most of the King's guard and stole her Grandfather's Core which allowed her to remember who the killer of her family was." He gives a smirk that unnerves Chaos. "Speaking of dear Alice, where is she?"

Chaos cannot believe his ears and searches Anthony's face for any sign of a joke. Alice's blood drenches the air so much so that Chaos is sure that even Edgar can smell her blood.

"Right behind you on the ground," Chaos says, gesturing with his head towards Alice.

Anthony turns slowly and almost deliberately towards the tree. He sighs and bends down. Chaos sees him whisper something in her ear. He hefts her up and Chaos sees how pale Alice truly became. Perhaps he overestimated the human's will? Humans are quite estranged for sure.

"I will be taking Alice back to the manor," Anthony says matter-of-factly. "She is in need of much medical treatment if her wounds are severe. If she can make it, that is." He sighs. "Perhaps you should have taken her Core earlier instead of letting her bleed, Chaos."

Anthony has only taken two steps when both Demons hear the jingle of bullets hitting each other. Before any could be loaded, the human male is on the ground, unconscious. Chaos barely caught the movement and stares in confusion at his once-friend.

"I do not appreciate your friend threatening me when I have done little to threaten him," Anthony states plainly. "Now, if you do not mind, I will be going."

Another few steps and this time Chaos steps in front of him.

Miss Alice

"That is my prize," Chaos says calmly. "Drop it and leave now or else I will kill you."

Chaos notes Anthony's sudden grip on Alice's arms.

"Humans have the same gender rules as we do," Anthony manages to say. "Alice is not an 'it.'"

Snorting, Chaos moves closer to Alice. "All humans are the same to me."

Soon the two Demons are nose-to-nose staring at each other. Both are searching for something in the other — a hint of movement, a plan of attack — but neither come up with anything. Chaos grins, though, as though finding something. Will Anthony call his bluff? Chaos highly doubts it.

"Clever boy," Chaos says. "But it will not work."

"I do not understand what you mean," Anthony replies calmly. "My only plan is to take her back to the manor."

"You are trying to trick me!" Chaos accuses.

"What trickery could I possibly do?" Anthony wonders. "What could I possibly accomplish from it?"

As Chaos ponders his next move Anthony manages another few steps.

"If you were trying to leave you would just go!" Chaos decides. Anthony sees some sign of paranoia in the estranged Demon's eyes and he cannot help but smile. "Why do you not run?"

"You seem unsteady on your feet, Chaos," Anthony claims. "Should I leave you unattended, who knows what you would do?"

"Why does it matter to you!?"

"It is dear Alice's manor," he states simply. "She would have my head if she woke to it in ruins."

"You fear the human, then?!"

132

Anthony sends a sharp look towards Chaos. In that look, Anthony tells that his actions have unsettled the Demon. Should he count it as a blessing or a curse? Chaos looks ready to bolt but, at the same time, looks ready to lash out. Which will he do first?

"Perhaps I fear her," Anthony admits, "but I know she can do no harm to me."

"Do you never tire of her insistent yelling?"

For the first time in the conversation, Anthony cannot answer his question. Yes, he has tired of her yelling, of her harsh words and scolds, but what of those times when her yelling was not for anger? Those rare times at events when Alice is happy, or when she would run around the house to escape Lady Belle, playing some estranged version of tag. Every time Alice would go to the town, to the pastry chef, those times of blatant happiness where her voice would raise but never in malice or spite. Did Anthony tire of those times as well? He feels unsure. He finds humans in general tiresome but...had Alice not been that exception for him?

Chaos misreads his hesitation. He must be hesitating because he does not want to admit it! Obviously, that must be it! Instantly, Chaos jumps to it, closing the space and snaking his arms under Alice's body.

"Let me take the burden off your shoulders," Chaos insists. "I promise you, you will feel better. You will have a seat by my throne, as well. Just give it to me."

Anthony looks up in the sky, smiles coldly and then looks at Chaos for a second more.

"I told you once before, Chaos," Anthony says. "Alice is a girl."

Anthony throws Alice in the air, and when Chaos looks up he sees an unfamiliar face. He takes in the woman's frail body, sunken face, and most importantly, her black, torn wings. He curses under his breath before looking at Anthony with malice.

133

"What is this?" he demands as the woman lands. "Why is she here?!"

"I hate this fool as much as the next Demon," Serene says, holding Alice carefully in her arms now, "but I care for the poor human he betrayed more." She grins wickedly. "Besides, I did not have much else to do after you left the barrier and you left me jobless. Maybe this will get me back into the collecting business."

"Serene, go," Anthony says. He does not turn to them, refuses to turn to them.

One day, many years ago, at a party with the many neighboring rulers, one Lord asked Alice if she wanted to change anything that happened in her past. Alice had not hesitated to tell the Lord, "If I wanted to change anything I would first have to have regrets. The events of the past are sad, yes, but I grew and learned from them. As such, I have no regrets. Thus, I would not change anything." Many people were surprised by her claim, Anthony being one of them. He had assumed that Alice's past would hold many regrets, but, perhaps, not all humans are the same. Anthony had never taken her words to heart, if he truly had something like a heart, but he thinks he understands them now.

If he turns around now, he will want to change his decision. Why change what you cannot fix or alter? Grow and learn from those mistakes, as Alice had said.

For a long minute Serene expects Anthony to say something else, but he does not even look in their direction. Alice moans in her arms so, sparing a single glance at Anthony, she leaves them just as silently as she came.

Once she is back in the manor Serene looks back out the window.

"Goodbye, you fool," Serene whispers before calling for the help. Every person in the manor seems to react simultaneously and Alice is whisked away from her.

Just a moment before the door shuts, she hears Alice whisper something to one of the doctors. He looks back at Serene but she cannot answer him.

"What happened to Anthony?"

After the door closes and Serene is left in the wake of the event, in the stillness and silence, she attempts to understand the human's question. Serene had not heard anger in the human's voice. Why she had not been angry Serene cannot fathom. What Serene heard in its place made it all much more confusing: worry. Pure, untainted worry.

Chapter 15

Chaos runs through the scarce woods behind Alice's manor, his furry making him more and more confused. He turns in circles and yells at the trees, unaware as to where his opponent lays.

Anthony sits in a tree, watching Chaos run around like a fool, waiting until the perfect time. Darkness blankets the land, the moon covered with sparse clouds. A chill is in the air, enough for breath to be seen. Barely a whisper of wind or of small animals. All the lights at Alice's manor have been extinguished and Anthony knows, without a doubt, Alice could never get out of the manor now. If she did manage to get out with her injuries she would be pulled back in almost instantly. He highly doubts she could get past Serene anyways.

So, falling without the slightest whisper to the ground, Anthony waits for Chaos to notice him. When he does, Chaos hardly blinks before he is grappling the other Demon to the ground. Anthony can see the shimmer where other creatures appear from Chaos's rage but none know what to do.

Anthony slices through the other man's shirt, scraping bone and tearing down his arm as he jumps back. Chaos howls, angry at being hit. His red eyes glow in the dark, a beacon for anyone to see. Small sprite-like creatures pull at Anthony's hair, skin and clothes but he easily swats them away.

"Where did that Harpy take my prize?!" bellows Chaos. "Where is it?!"

With two brisk steps, Anthony goes to punch Chaos in the jaw but the Demon dances back enough so that he only manages to be clipped. Chaos staggers back and continues to glare at Anthony.

"Alice is neither a prize nor an 'it,'" states Anthony. "I do not comprehend why you are trying to steal her away from me. After all, you did promise me the strongest of the line."

"Had I known Alice's Core was going to be this powerful then I would have promised the second strongest!" he yells. "That Core is far too valuable to be given to scum like you."

"So I am the scum," Anthony says casually. "Perhaps you have not looked in the mirror."

Chaos opens his mouth to reply but Anthony comes behind him, kicks right behind the knee, catching Chaos's head between his hands. Chaos snorts, as though ashamed of the hold. Although surprised he did expect more from Anthony.

"A simple snap of the neck will only minimize the problem," he states. "Attack the heart in my chest, Anthony. I know you have it in you so go on! Solve your problems for Alice's life time, perhaps even her children's life time." When Anthony remains silent Chaos laughs. "Wonderful! The puny human has changed you far too much, Anthony."

Without warning, Chaos latches his fingers inside of Anthony's sides. Cursing, Anthony tries to push him away but to little avail. Chaos stands up and smacks his head back. Anthony stumbles backwards and rests on a tree, hand on his head while he tries to focus on his surroundings.

"Without your damsel you are not much of a fight," Chaos coos. He grabs Anthony's arm and twists it around. "See how much that *hurts*?" He twists harder and hears a satisfying crunch followed by Anthony's brief yell. "And you do not even receive the rejuvenation benefits as I did. How *lucky*."

Tugging at his arm, Chaos spins Anthony off the tree and slams him on the ground, pinning him thoroughly to the ground with his knees. Chaos leans a good portion of his weight into Anthony's cracked shoulder and takes pure bliss in hearing him yell out.

"Oh but is this not *fun*?" Chaos asks. "Before the barrier incident, remember how much fun we would have? Humans were no match for us then and they never will be. So, tell me, why are you fighting for them now?"

Why indeed? Why bother protecting Alice, who has yelled at him and no longer wants anything to do with him? Why help her be free of being hunted from Chaos when she had so willingly given up? Why does he want to help Alice when she would not even let Anthony complete their contract? Anthony cannot answer any of them.

"I refuse to let you take or harm Alice," Anthony finally says through gritted teeth, "because our contract was never fulfilled."

For just a brief moment, Chaos lets up on Anthony's shoulder but, all too soon, the pressure is back and with a stronger force.

"You said she discovered who the murderer was," he snarls.

"Seems like your research was not complete," Anthony mocks.

Ignoring his comment, Chaos growls, "What else was in your contract?"

Anthony is about to give a retort but Chaos plows on without him.

"Of course, whether or not you tell me it will not matter," Chaos tells him triumphantly. "As soon as you are terminated the contract will be broken. Alice will have no defense and—"

Compiling all his strength in one movement, Anthony manages to roll over, crushing his shoulder beneath his own weight but freeing himself nonetheless. Both Demons stand and glare at each other but Anthony wobbles slightly. Gritting his teeth Anthony takes two steps to get closer to Chaos but is stopped midway through his second step. He feels needle pricks along his body and, when he looks up, can barely make out five or six floating orbs.

Chaos laughs hysterically. "If you had been here this whole time you would have been prepared, you damned fool!"

"What?" demands Anthony.

More and more of the orbs appear, circling Chaos in a mad dance.

"My latest creation, of course!" he yells, red eyes dancing with glee. "My Fate Weavers. They can control anybody or anything, living or dead. Is that not just wonderful?" Chaos strides over and gets in his face. "Now that you are incapable of moving, perhaps we should proceed."

He steps away and after a moment turns to look at Edgar who stands on shaky legs.

"Edgar, he is yours," Chaos says flippantly. "I need to find my prize."

Anthony cannot yell or curse, cannot grit his teeth or stomp. He barely has his thoughts, which are cluttered with intensifying pain and panic. Serene had promised she would stay with Alice until she was healed but what fear would holding a promise to a dead man bring? Anthony could only hope she would keep her word.

"I have waited far too long for this," Edgar states. His eyes focus and he holds up his gun. "A bullet or four through the heart should do nicely, would it not? Maybe a bullet for each year Rowan had been alive. No we have no such time. I guess only one or two through the heart will have to do."

Anthony feels the gun press against his chest but barely registers it in his mind.

"Point blank range will be a bit messy," Edgar grumbles. "But it is the surest way to kill you."

He hears the shot but it does not register as pain. He hears a second and third and barely has time to register the ground before it is in his face. He registers very little, knowing he will soon be sent to the lowest portions of whatever hellhole he is worthy of. He will have to start from the very bottom and work his way up again.

Why would he bother risking so much for such a silly little human? Anthony thinks he understands now. What drove him to protect her, to come back and make sure she would be protected after his fall. She had said it to him, perhaps in anger, but it had impacted him more than anything else.

The silly little human called him a friend.

Before he closes his eyes, he turns to look up at the night sky. His shoulder and abdomen barely flicker with pain but his chest throbs and burns with a pain worse than anything he had ever felt before. He hears someone coming but does not look their way. He figures it is probably Edgar or Chaos, making sure he was really going away and not just playing opossum.

Someone nudges his shoulder and a brief flicker of pain runs through him but it does not concern him. He hears something swish close to him. Of course the wind would pick up now. Perhaps rain will come soon.

Pale light washes over everything. Is it the moon or failing vision?

Anthony blinks slowly and it seems to take much longer than it should. When his eyes open again, he sees Alice looking down at him with a mixture of too many emotions. What is she doing here? She is pale, injured, and could easily catch a cold. She should be inside.

He tries to tell her that but she does not seem to understand. She slams her hand against his face twice and he sees her looking very angry now. How strange. He sees Serene's face as she tries to grab Alice but Alice pushes Serene away. Serene looks shocked, maybe by what Alice says. Alice tries to tell Anthony something but she is too quiet.

He manages to tell Alice, "Good night, Miss Alice," but he is unsure if she heard him.

Oh what a joy it would bring Anthony if that worry in her face was directed towards him.

Chapter 16

Alice fully awakens not too long after the doctors on hand patch her together to the best of their abilities. The sun has almost set and only a candle gives her any form of light. After some time Alice became only slightly aware of her wounds, her mind distracted in attempts at comprehension.

Anthony had done his damage and had no reason to come back to her so what are his motives? Obviously he must have been trying to hold a debt over her head. Alice hates owing someone anything. With this debt Alice would not be able to just let him leave. After all, he had practically saved her life to some extent. Something about her theory feels wrong though. Alice looks around but she does not see Anthony. She remembers him but she also remembers another face.

Pulling back her blanket with her unhurt arm she cringes at the pull in her side and wobbles to her feet. Alice shakily walks to the door and opens it. A blast of cold air hits her face and Alice looks around. Her shoulder starts to throb but she pushes past it. Her mind drifts towards the pain in her shoulder more and more until she spots someone.

At first Alice is sure it is Anthony but, after a moment, she shakes her head. It is a woman, no doubt, and almost bird like in frailty. Alice staggers over to the woman and sits down to rest and catch her breath.

"You are the one who brought me home," Alice states a tad breathlessly. "You must know where Anthony is then."

"I would like to say dead but that will not be happening for a while," she says. "I can hear them in the woods. They will be at it for a while."

Alice snorts and sends a sharp look towards the bird-like woman. "Anthony is a Demon. It is impossible for him to die."

"You have been living with a Demon for years and can still use the word 'impossible' so lightly," the woman mutters. "Perhaps humans do not change as much as I thought they did."

"Those are not my words," Alice snaps. "Anthony told me himself. Demons do not die."

"You still hold his words to truth?" the woman asks. "Years you have been together and yet you were never aware that the man who killed your family was right in front of your nose? Yet you still hold to his word. How ridiculously pathetic."

"If you are not immortal then a shot to the head or heart should end you correct?"

At that, the woman turns sharply to look at Alice. Alice's glare, unyielding as she stares at the woman, composed and determined despite everything that had happened.

"A shot in the heart would kill any Demon but a mere human could not get a shot easily, as I am sure you know."

"But Demons do not die." Alice glares at the bird-like woman while she searches the human's face. Alice's anger...why does it point so strongly towards her and not Anthony? Not the Demon who has betrayed her but the one who is protecting her.

"Should a Demon's heart be destroyed, it causes them to be sent to the Demon King's barrier. There he will be judged by the Demon King and his fate determined. As such, it is possible for a Demon to die but it is quite unlikely."

"Why would you claim that Anthony would be dead then?" Alice demands.

"What, are you still half dead?" the woman snaps. "You were in the possession of Chaos and his human puppets and Anthony came to your rescue. He is still there. Can you not put two and two together?"

"You are a fool if you think Anthony would die by those two," Alice remarks. "He has gotten through worse unscathed."

"At least I am seeing clearly." The woman looks towards the woods, where she hears Anthony taunt Chaos, hears a small scuffle, before Chaos yells in anger at losing sight of Anthony again. "Anthony has no intentions of coming back, you idiot. Why do you think I am here?"

"Anthony is away from the manor. I am a weak human close to death. The obvious answer is my Core. Though if you were here for my Core, you would have taken it while I was asleep, unless you, like Chaos, prefers to make a show. You do not strike me as the flashy kind of woman. Perhaps a friend of Anthony? No, your immediate wish for his death would mean something else. Perhaps a crossed-friend but not an enemy nor a simple acquaintance. Whoever and whatever you are, I would rather not address you as 'woman' and would ask of your name."

"My name is Serene," Serene replies tightly. "What, has Anthony bothered to mention me in the past?"

"No, but you are much like the human lords here," Alice replies. "Easy to read and simple-minded."

"You are a spoiled child," snaps Serene.

"Please, think of an original insult if you wish to criticize me."

Without even a thought, Serene's stretched and torn wings fly from her back, blocking out the setting sun and Serene reaches down to yank up the human. Holding Alice by the free material of her white dress, Serene glares at the child and resists the urge to throw her to the moon.

Miss Alice

Alice raises her uninjured arm and slaps Serene hard enough for Serene to stumble and release her grip on the human. Balancing herself, Alice stares at the creature in front of her.

"My guess is a Harpy, correct?" Alice asks casually. "A half-bird, half-woman creature. In human myths, Harpies are known to lead males from their path. If that is true, were you just randomly picked as a Harpy or was it a deliberate thing?"

Serene stares up at Alice, more than a little shocked to see the human appearing curious and a little bored.

"I could have snapped your neck," Serene says, holding her cheek. She hopes Alice cannot see how much the slap had hurt.

"But you did not," Alice replies. "You are here for something other than my Core, obviously. Assuming that you are a crossed-friend, I have to wonder about your involvement. You should have no reason to assist Anthony – unless, of course, you are in alliance with Chaos." Serene scowls deeply and Alice laughs. "No need for that kind of a face, Serene; I am just throwing options in the open. So humor me. Why are you here?"

"Anthony asked for my assistance," she states. "Asked me to protect you until you are healthy again."

"I assume there is more to the story," Alice says. "Getting only half of the story is not nearly as fun. By how you are referring to him, I would guess that your relationship is not the best. Crossed-friend is the best guess and, if that is true, you should not be willing to help him. What did he promise you, I wonder? Or did he beg to protect his little human? Perhaps he figured that he would come back for my Core if you were to keep me safe. He would help you gain in power, perhaps move up in whatever social order you Demons have."

Refusing to say anything, Serene stands there, staring at the human girl oddly. Anthony must have told her something of them if she knows all of this, but how much? Hardly enough of the story but perhaps a large sum of it?

"He promised no such reward," Serene confides. "He asked for assistance for someone else, which is quite unusual in and of itself. Perhaps I was curious to meet the human girl so many claimed to be fearsome."

Alice snorts. "I doubt the latter. As for the rest…I guess I will have to take it." She pauses and then stands unsteadily. Serene takes a step towards Alice but she waves Serene off. "Do not concern yourself with me. If you wish to help me or protect me, then let me know when Chaos is coming." Alice walks towards the manor's entrance, catching herself every few steps.

Confused, Serene starts to walk behind Alice once she is halfway to the door. "How do you know Chaos will come to you?" she asks. "You have faith in Anthony, why do you not consider he will kill Chaos?"

"People who are compared to hunting dogs do not simply give up," Alice replies flatly. *What a shame, my intentions to see hunting dogs before a time like this were in order to verify Anthony's claims. Anthony should have kept his grimy hands off Grandfather's Core for another day or so.* She sighs and grabs the handle to the door. "Besides, Serene, you said it yourself: Demons cannot die."

As they enter the manor little is said. Alice moves quietly enough while Serene sifts through the house silently. Alice leads the way, pausing every few steps to catch her breath before hurrying along. By the time they reached the Show Room the sun has set and Alice is struggling to move more than two or three steps at a time.

Collapsing in a chair, Serene shuts the door and lights the candles around the room. Once Alice has managed to catch her breath she goes over to the drawer with the ten or more guns inside. She grabs one, frowns, and reaches for another. Serene can barely tell the difference in the metallic weapons and goes to question Alice about it when Serene whips her head towards the window. Faintly she can hear Edgar and Chaos talking.

"Alice," Serene says, not looking away from the window. "I fear you have less time than I first thought."

145

"I assume Chaos is on the way," Alice replies breathlessly. She pulls out a single gun and places it on the table. "Do not fret for me. Make sure everyone else in the manor is away."

"I am to keep you safe," Serene reminds her. "I cannot do that if I am not with you."

After a moment, Alice asks, "Was it a promise?"

"Why does it matter?"

"Just answer me."

"Yes. Anthony made me promise that I would keep you safe and within my sights until you were healed."

Smiling, Alice stands and squares her shoulders against the pain radiating through her. "Anthony must have finally understood. How sad. Well, for once I am willing to let someone break a promise." Alice steels her gray eyes on Serene's red and Serene is surprised by the look she sees. Determination with a mixture of glee and anger. "You trusted Anthony for whatever reason when he came to you. I am asking you to trust me as well. I will not die here Serene; I can promise you that."

"What good is the promise of a dead man?" Even as she speaks the words, Serene is moving towards the door. She had asked Anthony the same thing, although his answer was certainly more necessary than Alice's. As Anthony had no intentions of returning, Serene had been hesitant to accept his request. His answers had been the deciding factor for Serene. Although unnecessary now, she is curious for the human's answer.

"It is not a dead man's promise if the man does not die," Alice replies and places a bullet inside the gun. "You will hear one shot. Come back when that shot is heard. Until then, do not come back. Otherwise, that bullet will go to you."

Serene leaves the room and only after she has redirected the entire manor's help back to their rooms does she realize the oddity of what she is doing. She grins incredulously and admiringly. A human, so assured and completely without fear when going against someone such as Chaos – a human thrust into this maddening world, so calm and collected. How strange, Serene is not particularly worried about Alice's safety, surprising considering her enemy. What a peculiar little human indeed.

Back in the Show Room Alice sits at the table, facing the window, now open to the world. A cool breeze floats in, allowing the faint sound of a shot to resound even to Alice's ears. Her shoulder aches, her side throbs, and all Alice wants to do is sleep but she keeps her posture taught as if waiting for an important Lord.

"Has anyone ever told you not to leave your windows open? You may let monsters inside."

Chaos appears in the room soon after his voice. Alice does not jump but stands and gestures towards the chair.

He chuckles. "I should not be surprised to see you moving so soon after such a horrible wound. But, alas Alice, you have indeed baffled me once again." He takes a single look at the gun in the center of the table and stares at Alice curiously. "Most humans would have that pointed at me."

"I am ashamed that you would consider me in the group of 'most humans'," Alice replies. "Please, sit. I believe you will enjoy what I have to say."

"Oh, I am sure I will," Chaos replies, taking a seat. Alice follows soon after and he stares at her with a wide grin. "What do you wish to say to me, Alice?"

"Have you ever read the story about the young man, the tiger, and the fair princess?"

Blinking in confusion, Chaos says, "I believe I have, once. Quite an unsatisfying read."

"Then have you ever played a game of roulette?"

"The gambling game or the risk game?"

Miss Alice

"I believe both apply to this game," Alice replies. "We will take turns, Chaos. See who is worthy to walk out that door, to meet the fair princess. The other, well, they will take their fate with the ferocious tiger." Alice picks up the gun and studies it, pointing it straight at Chaos's heart. "You will point the gun to your chest, pull the trigger and, if you should survive, you will ask me a question. I will answer honestly and then take the gun, point it at my head, pull the trigger, and ask you a question. Of course, you will answer honestly in return."

Chaos's grin widens. "You have developed a risky mind, Alice," he says.

"Then you accept the game?"

He nods. "Only, it does not seem quite fair. Should you die I do not receive my prize. I would be the loser either way."

"Perhaps, Chaos, you should simply react faster."

Alice watches as Chaos's grin turns to laughter. He takes the gun and holds it oddly.

"What is stopping me from lying, or shooting you now?" he asks.

"What is the point in lying to someone who is bound to lose?" Alice replies. "Should you shoot me dead you will be losing your precious prize. You get first question."

Throwing his head back for another laugh Chaos points the gun to his heart and pulls the trigger. A soft click and then Chaos sighs overdramatically.

"And here I was worried for a moment," he says sarcastically. "So, Alice, I get any question that you must answer honestly. So many questions, too little time. Only five slots left." He pauses for a moment then smiles. "What is driving you to defy me, instead of just giving me your Core? After all, your ultimate defeat is at hand."

Reaching across the table, Alice grabs the gun and takes it in her hand.

"For spite," Alice replies. "You wish to control my life and I refuse to let that happen." Holding the gun to her head, Alice pulls the trigger with a straight face. "When you die, you are sent to your King to be judged. How does he judge those who come to him?"

Frowning, Chaos takes the gun from Alice's outstretched hand. "From what I remember he would base it on what they have done. Any broken laws would be accounted for and scaled on his or her accomplishments and power status. A fickle process that changes slightly depending on the person being judged." Placing the gun against his chest, Chaos hesitates for a split second before pulling the trigger. "Humans are attached to their Cores very deeply and seem to consider the emotions in their bodies as being alive. Alice, I do not believe you are one of those who agree with that notion. You are very different than the other humans I have met. Alice, what do you see as living?"

Taking the gun from Chaos's hand, Alice smiles tightly. "Every small and humble thing makes the world beautiful. To fully comprehend that, you must understand the joy that simplicity can bring. To feel joy, you must have a Core and have experienced calamity. If I understand their purpose correctly only a Core can allow a human to experience such things." Alice raises her arm and points the gun to her temple. Closing her eyes, she hears the soft click and then slides it across the table. "Why did you want Anthony to rule beside you?"

Surprise flickers on Chaos's face as he grabs the gun with a shaking hand. He meets Alice's gaze steadily for a second before looking away. She appears very assured and confident. She even appears *gloating*. Only two slots left and if he gets away from this shot, she will be dead. Why gloat now, before the end?

"We shared common goals and mindsets," Chaos says. "He was different from the other Demons I met. Not to mention we were brought into existence again at the same time." He stares at the gun warily. He should not be worried but something knots his stomach. He feels the need to stall but he knows such a feat is impossible for much longer.

"How about a change of rules," Alice pipes in. "You can ask me a question before you pull the trigger. Should you live this next round, you can take my Core and my life."

"Why bother with the sudden rule change?" Chaos asks, officially on edge. "What would either benefit?"

"Was it not you who said that dying ignorantly is the worst of deaths?" Alice responds. "You should be happy to know that I will not count either of the two questions you just asked me. Although the next question you ask will."

Breathing steadily, Chaos stares at her composed figure. Unfazed by her possibly imminent death or even injuries. *Is her face a ruse, or is she truly this confident?* Chaos cannot understand her and cannot begin to understand her.

Finally Chaos asks, "Why?"

"What a loaded question," Alice replies. "I believe, though, that the best answer is perhaps one of the most overlooked answers all Demons seem to misunderstand. Why do I do this? Why do I care so much for my Core? Why play this game? Why go on living? Honestly, I am saddened you have not seen it yet, Chaos." He glares at Alice and Alice smiles. "My answer Chaos is remarkably uncomplicated: because I am human. We are a species so simple we appear complicated, but one thing we do better than any other is be underestimated."

Chaos opens his mouth to question her but he thinks better of himself. He picks up the gun and in his head he tells himself that it is a blank shot; that Alice has sent herself to her doom but he cannot believe it. Alice has played her cards and has an extra ace in her sleeve. Even if this shot was blank, something will happen; somehow she will gain the upper-hand.

He lifts the gun to his chest and, after collecting his wits, pulls the trigger.

Chaos falls to the ground, eyes wide and confused. Alice walks over and stands above him.

"How?" he demands.

She makes a *tsk-tsk* noise at him and then laughs, holding the gun out for him to see. She shows him inside the barrel, the *five* slots.

"Breaking the rules at the brink of death," she says in a chiding tone. "How unprofessional." She tosses the gun aside and crouches down to his level. "You should have spun it yourself or checked the gun once you had it in your hands. Even you should know that, if the barrel is spun all the way, the heavier slot will land at the bottom due to gravity's pull. Although I could not be for sure, once I got past my second turn I knew I was safe."

"This is neither the ending nor goodbye I foresaw," Chaos claims.

"Why do you assume this is an ending?" Alice asks. "I am sure we will see one another again."

Serene comes in and is shocked to see Chaos on the ground, a hole in his chest and Alice staring at him like he is the most curious thing she has ever met.

"Hello Serene," Alice says as she stands. "We should be off. Not much time left, I would imagine."

"To do what?" Serene asks, her shock quickly moving into confusion. How had she managed to get in that close to shoot his heart? How had Chaos not blocked the attack?

Chaos laughs painfully. "You silly Harpy," he says with a smile. "Take her to Anthony already."

"I am afraid to say you will have to carry me," Alice says. "I highly doubt we will be able to make it before...well, before whatever happens to Demons that end like that." She gestures towards Chaos, who laughs and cringes at the same time. "Until next time, Chaos." She curtsies and then leaves with Serene.

Chapter 17

Alice and Serene find Anthony mere seconds before he is taken back to the Demon King's barrier. They are taken as well, the gargoyles unsure which is Demon and which is human. Alice's shoulder wound opened again as she was placed inside her cell.

"I cannot believe the disrespect of this place!" Alice grumbles as two ghostly women come to her to fix the wound. "Honestly, you would think the King of Demons would have some respect for me. At least Chaos kept everything orderly and respectful. Ow!" She glares at the ghostly women who float back a little before returning to Alice's arm.

"You should be thankful he did not have us killed," Serene snaps. "And you are certainly not one to be judging on respect, anyways."

"At least I can keep a guest happy when I need to," Alice replies.

A gargoyle crawls in, creeping along the floor much like a cat compared to the others she had seen. He comes to the bars and looks at Alice flatly. Only after the two women patch Alice up again and leave does the gargoyle speak to them.

"The King wish audience with human," the creature says. "Harpy come, sure."

Standing up, Serene is slightly behind Alice who appears much more confident than Serene could even imagine being in such a situation. Although Serene knows very little about the Demon King, having only met him on one other occasion, what is there to

Sarah Gastright

really know? He is not known to be kind or forgiving. Fair and cruel are the trademarks that most if not all Demons knows him for.

When coming into a giant room, a huge throne sits on top of a hill of stairs. Serene and Alice stumble back a few steps at the brightness of the room. Everything is in black and red, dark colors that seem to devour any light, but the stairs and the frame of the giant throne are set with millions of jewels, primarily of clear diamonds, deep red rubies and dark onyx. In the top of the room is the sun and moon, the glass ceiling causing a harsh glare. Both Anthony and Chaos lay on the top stairs with a scale over their heads, nothing on them but the plates have already moved. What catches Alice's attention most is the King himself.

"Welcome!" he says. "You must be Alice, the human."

Frowning, Alice can barely keep all her thoughts from becoming words. "Are you the King?" she asks.

He nods and bows deeply. "And you are the Queen, though of different worlds."

"You are barely older than ten!" Alice exclaims, irritated.

"Twelve, really, is my outwards age," he replies. "Are you surprised that someone younger than yourself could ever rule a whole kingdom?"

"I highly doubt you are truly twelve nor were you placed as King when you were twelve," Alice grumbles. "I am still younger."

He laughs and hurries down the steps. At the bottom he grabs Alice's good arm and pulls her up the steps, stopping her two steps away from the two Demons lying unconscious. Serene is stopped at a platform five steps below Alice.

Alice could have mistaken the Demon King to be a normal kid. Untidy brown hair in need of a cut, with strands of hair falling into his face, and skin of boys who spend too much time outside. He has a red cape tied around his neck and a tailored black suit on. A scepter which he twirls around, fast and blurring with far too much practice. Of course, his eyes are what remind Alice that he cannot be *normal*. They change color, drifting from red to blue to black to gold and everything in between. Alice is fascinated by his eyes, curious as to why they change color.

"These are from my own Demon gene pool but I only got them as part of the packaged deal," the King says, stopping the top of his scepter just below his left eye. "Not only do I get to rule all Demons, live in an amazing mansion, and get anything that I ever want but I get an amazing power boost, which led to these fantastic eyes! When I am not twirling this stupid thing I am looking in a mirror." He shakes his head but keeps a mischievous grin up. "Anyways, Alice, what brings you to my humble abode?"

"Just grabbed a gargoyle and decided to pay a house visit," Alice replies blandly, causing the King to chuckle. Alice points at Anthony, setting her glare on the King. "I need him back."

"Oh? What for?"

"We never completed our contract."

He laughs again. "Alice, ignorant Alice, once a Demon is brought here before my feet, all contracts are terminated. Any other reason you desire this Demon back? Are you aware of how many rules he has broken? He should be destroyed right this instant. Along with that one." He gestures towards Chaos.

"I agree," Alice says, making the King's eyebrows shoot up in surprise. "Both deserve a fate worse than simple destruction. I think we can make a fair enough deal to work both sides."

"I am very interested," the King says, smiling. "I hardly ever have humans here, Alice. I am excited to see what your race can do on its own."

"Turn Anthony back into a human," Alice says. "I will have total control over him and he can live out many years in punishment and exile. Eventually, you can have him return to here to be judged once again. If, by then, everything that he has done wrong still outweighs what he has endured as punishment, he can be destroyed. Otherwise he will be placed back into his position as a Demon."

"I only see this working in favor of you, Alice," the King states. "Do you simply assume I can turn a Demon into human? Are you sure that is even possible? Even if he was turned human, how could you ever hope to control him? Certainly not by Core, something which humans cannot hold in their hands."

Gesturing towards Chaos, Alice says, "He created a new creature called Fate Weavers. They could turn any living or nonliving object into puppets at his control. Change some small details in them and it would be very possible to control a human or Demon."

"That does not answer the other questions, though."

"I do not see why it could not be possible. Statues can fly, nightmares walk the streets and Demons help humans. Thinking of a Demon turning into a human is not hard to believe when compared to the rest of the world."

"So you want me to turn Anthony into a human that you have control over through modified Fate Weavers."

"He will still have free will, of course. He will be my servant but under heavier restrictions which could be discussed at a later time. Should those be violated, he will endure a slight shock by my hand."

"And after so long he will be judged again. Should his negativity still outweigh his positivity, he will be destroyed on the spot. Vice versa and he will be resumed back as a Demon as though nothing ever happened."

"You get the pleasure of seeing a strong Demon forced into servitude as a mere human." Alice grins wickedly. "As the superior race, how much of a blow would that do to be placed at a lower standard?"

A long pause stretches out and the King watches Alice skeptically. He has heard of the strange human through many tales but had hardly believed any of them to be true. He has never come

155

across a human like this in any of the years he was with them. He looks at the two Demons on the floor in front of him, at Alice and then grins at the ceiling.

"Can I recruit you as a Demon?" the King asks, turning his smile to Alice. "Pretty please? I need someone like you on my side."

"That very well depends on how well this goes over," Alice replies, returning his smile. "I was certain that I would be going to Hell once I die anyways."

He bellows with laughter and then grabs her hand tightly, putting his scepter to the side.

"I like you, Alice," he says. "I would love to see how this goes over. Oh, but I must ask. What shall I do with the other one?" He gesture towards Chaos carelessly. "He was such a good fellow. Shame to see him fall to this."

From the back Serene is surprised by their talk. Never in her life would she have thought that their King could be so...childish. She had thought he him a hard, cruel man who yelled much and would never let a human talk to him on equal grounds. Every Demon has surely thought the same thing or at least most of them.

Eventually, Alice and the King reach an agreement. The King would work on the Fate Weavers and returning Anthony to a much more human state. As long as Anthony kept to being a good citizen under Alice's ruling, he would do fine. Their time limit would be Alice's natural life. He would visit on some occasions to see how things are going, but would otherwise leave it to Alice.

"As for the Harpy," he yells with a grin on his face. "I see I misjudged the events that happened so short a-time ago. I would like to offer my deepest apologies and, Serene, a job offer."

"Sir?" Serene asks, surprised she had not stumbled over the simple word.

"No need for such formalities," he says, brushing away the title with a wave of his scepter. "For this assignment, I would like you to be my messenger and watch over this one" – he kicks

Anthony in the arm – "when I cannot. As an apology for my incorrect judgment, I would like to give you your position as a collector back as well. Does this seem fair to you?"

Nodding, Serene nearly bounces over and hugs the King but she restrains herself. "You are very gracious," she says. "Thank you very much."

"For now, please return to your manor, Alice," he says. "Serene, if you would please continue to watch over her. It should not be for long and Anthony shall be returned to you soon."

With proper handshake to seal the deal, Alice and the King say goodbyes with matching wicked grins. Serene chuckles in wonder and, as she walks back to the manor with Alice in her arms, she wonders about the future. Will Alice become a Demon herself? Favored, for sure, by the King.

Alice is bombarded by her help almost as soon as she steps into her home. They ask how she is, they want to help her to bed, bring her food, change her bandages. Serene laughs at the unhappy face Alice makes as they tell her to rest and not to strain herself.

As night settles down, Serene pokes her head into Alice's room.

"Alice, may I ask you a question?" Serene asks.

Nodding, Alice sits up in her bed, waiting for Serene to continue.

"When you were with Chaos, I could hear some of what you said," she tells Alice. "I know the game and deciphered the rules that you had in play. Did you really know that you would not get the bullet?"

"There was always that chance," Alice replies. "But I never break my promises. I was lucky to have picked the fair maiden instead of the tiger."

"You were not afraid of the King, then?"

"Hardly! A boy like that is not to be feared! Not with his young face, at least."

Serene laughs. "One more question, if you do not mind." Alice nods and Serene takes a moment to steel herself. "You changed Anthony. I am not sure how but, when I first heard about his whole plan, I had thought to pity you." Alice glares at Serene who looks everywhere but Alice. "Whatever you do, Alice, you change perspectives of people. The man who came to rescue you and the one who asked me for help are not the same men."

"You have not asked a question yet," Alice says sharply.

"How, then? How did you turn Anthony from the Demon I knew him as to what he is now? How did you stay so confident under the risky game you played with Chaos? How did you keep a straight face with the King?"

"More than one question," Alice states, then gives a tight smile. "Humans are highly underestimated when they go against another species. Use that to your advantage and you are bound to see them slip. It is quite easy once you figure out their pattern."

"I have not slipped," Serene replies stiffly.

"I managed to slap you," Alice reminds her. "Had you not underestimated me as a human, taking me as an equal, you would not have let that happen. Do not feel too bad, Serene. Anthony has slipped more times than you." Alice regains her glare at Serene who looks at her feet. "If I could, you would be slapped equal times for daring to even consider pitying me. I need no pity from the likes of you, of Lords, or anyone else."

Chuckling nervously, Serene manages to pull her eyes to Alice. She cannot help but wonder, just for a moment, what goes on in the human's head, what makes her tick. Still, this is certainly not a good time to ask. Serene is wary of tripping some unbeknownst wire.

"Be well, Alice," Serene says, taking her leave.

Serene walks down the long hallway and comes into a Sitting Room, where a large portion of the help are sitting. Some are resting, some chatting and only a few look up when Serene enters the room.

"Miss," one asks cautiously. Serene looks at the younger girl in curiosity and she shuffles around nervously. "Is the Princess doing well?"

"Idiot," another snaps. "She's the Queen now. The late King is on his deathbed."

Blushing, the first shuffles around a bit. "Is the young Queen well, then? Can you tell us what happened to her and what has become of Mister Anthony?"

Surprise flickers in Serene's stomach. "Alice is the Queen?" she asks.

All the help turn and look at her in surprise.

"Of course," the second, an older boy, says. "The last in the lineage right now. You must not be around here if you do not know the young Queen's face. She is well known in the town and most other kingdoms – for different reasons, of course, but still known."

"Anthony never told me that," Serene muses, then sighs. "Alice will be fine with some rest. I am quite sure that she will be moving around soon. As for Anthony... he should be returning soon."

"But what caused her to get such wounds?" the first asks. "You brought her back to us – twice for that matter! – so you must have been there or had seen what had happened!"

"Anthony gave her to me as I passed by," Serene tells them. "I saw nothing."

"Then what of the other shot we heard?" a third person asks. "When we came we saw no one in any room. Then you two appear at the brink of dawn – forgive me but you must understand our skepticism."

"I understand it perfectly," Serene tells them calmly. "Alice played a game of chance and, in the end, she proved victorious. She asked for my assistance in removing the body from the manor."

Many grumble in their protests but no one questions it. Serene hears them decide to ask Alice when she recovers.

"May I ask a question?" Serene asks, making the attention return to her. "I have not spent much time with Alice and from an outsider's view I cannot fathom why any of you stay here. There must be many of people who would hire such loyal and dedicated help?"

No one says anything for a while, as though considering the question deeply, before turning to the skittish girl who had spoken first.

"Princess— I mean, Queen Alice may not always be the most pleasant to be around," she says, darting her eyes towards the hallway, "but she has never once raised her hand at us. Perhaps she has yelled and scolded us but never raised a hand. She always placed the responsibility of our actions on Mister Anthony, as he is our manager. With our backgrounds, not many people would ever want us to help them so to think that the to-be Queen would have asked for our help was a miracle." She smiles kindly and the other slowly grow their own smiles, perhaps thinking of their own kind memories. "Despite her frosty face, I believe Queen Alice will be very benevolent and fair as our ruler."

Serene finds everything they are saying to be odd. She could never picture Alice as being benevolent.

"We must see different sides of the same coin," Serene admits. "I would never say that Alice would be benevolent. I can barely say she is pleasant to be around."

"It is hard to see if you look at her from face value," the second says. "You have known her during hard times so you must have only seen her cold side. Think past that, though. Has the young Queen endangered your life or any others except herself? I highly doubt it." Looking at her fellow workers, he asked, "Do you remember the time years ago when it was storming and the young Queen disappeared?" A few people nod their heads. He turns back to Serene. "The young Queen had gone outside during a horrible storm, Miss, and taken in travelers who had found their way to the crossroads. Mister Anthony had been quite unhappy with her and had argued with her for a very long time afterwards. Mudslides are quite common out that way but the young Queen had ignored him completely."

"She claimed that bringing them in would help people in the town like her more," the third says. "She even said that they had paid her. When some of us asked the travelers, they denied the latter and we believe that the former was simply a ruse. If that was true, why had she not taken others out with her or even sent some out to fetch them?" He shakes his head. "She can be quite a cold and harsh girl, really, but we believe she has a kind heart. You just have to look for it."

After that, Serene is ignored while the help simply gossips around, sharing stories of their wondrous young Queen Alice. Serene does not understand their reasoning and after a few more minutes of listening to them she walks out, moving around the house to make sure nothing more is coming. Eventually she settles in a guest room and stares out the window. She tries to understand the help's belief that Alice is truly a good, caring person but she cannot quite wrap her head around the idea.

"What a strange human," Serene says with a sigh. "She runs too quickly, even when blindfolded." She smiles. "Still, if the humans here believe she will be a good ruler, perhaps she will be. It will certainly be interesting."

Chapter 18

When Anthony blacked out, he did not know what to expect. Perhaps torture, maybe nothing at all? He had expected something to punish him for his multiple wrongdoings but nothing happened for the longest time. He could faintly hear voices but they made little sense to him. He felt as though he was merely asleep.

Then he kept seeing Alice. She would appear in his vision – or perhaps his mind – and then disappear. Each time with a different expression. Sometimes she would be hurt, other times fine.

Time passed and then he was reliving all the time with Alice. From the first time he led her away from her room to the time he passed her over to Serene. He thought it would end there, but it continued on. He saw her demanding another gargoyle to take her to the King and talking with the King. It continued so that Anthony was seeing events which he was not even present to see. He saw her playing her game with Chaos, her anger at the help for smothering her with care, and Serene's questions. He wonders if Alice will go to the town to pick up the silly pastries she loves so much or if she will stop now that she is Queen. He highly doubts she would stop that trend, no matter her position.

He feels someone shake him hard, and wonders if it is his imagination or not. Then he hears someone call his name and he frowns.

"You have to wake up now," a young boy says. "Come on, I know you are in there. Get up already."

Anthony tries to open his eyes, to move, but his whole body aches. Groaning, he pulls his eyes open and sees a young boy that looks vaguely familiar. It takes him a moment to realize the boy he is looking at is the King, the boy he had seen Alice talking to. Although he has never seen the Demon King before, he has the feeling that he has seen him other than in his visions of Alice's conversation with him.

"Can you sit up?" the King asks. "Try your best. You will need your strength back soon."

Somehow Anthony manages to sit up. He places a hand on his chest as it burns, as though he has run miles without break or held his breath far too long. He feels a dull throb in his shoulder but when he moves it he can tell that the primary injury is healed as well as the injuries in his sides. Only stiffness remains and he imagines that will pass with time.

The King thrusts a glass of water towards Anthony who takes it stiffly. Drinking causes more pain to sprawl through his body but he manages to withstand it enough to drink the whole glass.

"You have a very peculiar and loyal contracted," the King states flatly. "Never once has a human made such a deal without backing down. Never once have I felt as though I was talking to myself when talking to a human, either. You caught the double edged sword of contractors."

"What—" Anthony starts before breaking into a harsh cough, then cringes as his chest explodes in pain.

Sighing, the King comes over to him and frowns deeply. His ever-changing eyes are mesmerizing and almost hypnotic to Anthony and he cannot get over how young the King looks. He had expected an older looking fellow, someone who looked threatening.

"Talking will only make things worse right now," the King states. "This is my first attempt at such a thing. I am quite surprised your body held together. No, actually, I am not too surprised. You still had something that you enjoyed. Alice, was it not? Very interesting."

Anthony's cup is filled again and he drinks it quickly and he thinks the pain is diminishing.

"You are just as entranced by my eyes as Alice was," the King says. "It must have worked."

After a few more glasses, Anthony manages to speak without too many problems, although it still hurts to breathe.

"I do not understand," Anthony croaks.

"Your contracted – or, well, former contracted – struck a deal with me," the King states. "You will remain in her custody for her natural life and then will be judged again. After that, it is my decision as to how your fate will go from there." He grins wickedly, very close to the smiles Alice gives when discussing with a Lord, Anthony notices. "Perhaps I made this process much more painful than it should have been. My own form of justice."

"What...process?" Anthony manages. "Why am I not...dead?"

"What does Alice see in you?" the King mutters. "You are quite dimwitted. You are not dead because of Alice." The King grabs a large emblem and holds it in front of Anthony, who identifies it instantly. A Core, connected to a strange, shifting metal.

Unable to look away, Anthony tries to form a reasonable question but the King just laughs harshly at him.

"Can you still not understand?" he asks. "I have reverted you back to how you were before you became a Demon. I believe you will retain most of your reflexes but your muscles have greatly decayed. You will still be considered a strong and fast human but nowhere near what you used to be. I cannot say for certain about your reflexes as it is impossible to test those while you are half dead."

"How did you...make me human?" Anthony asks, perplexed. "That should be... impossible."

"To think you were once a Demon," the King sighs. "I manipulate time, Anthony. I control the time fluctuations between barriers and can even control time out of these barriers. In the simplest of ways of explaining, I have locked your body back in the time before you became a Demon, meaning it is only your perspective of time that has changed. I must emphasize the statement that your body is *locked* in time. Meaning, unless I unlock it, you will not be able to gain much more strength or speed unless I allow it. Your body is also much more fragile than before and pain receptors will be much more active. You are practically human. Do you understand?"

Nodding, Anthony looks at the child oddly. His eyes have been switching colors between deep red and shining black but suddenly change to bright blues, greens and grays.

"Well, I would like to tell you that you are quite lucky on the front that you did not end up like your friend," the King says in a sing-song voice. "Come see what he is going through, Anthony. I think you will approve nicely."

Without a second's delay the King jumps up and hurries to the door, tapping his foot impatiently as Anthony stumbles to catch up with the kid. They walk down a long hallway before coming to a glass wall. He looks inside and sees Chaos writhing on the floor, his mouth open in a silent scream.

"These walls are soundproof. King's secret," the King says. "He is being slowly decayed, starting with the tips of his fingers and toes. He will rot away; endure crushing pain as his bones are slowly being broken."

Anthony looks at the King, at his bright and excited face, and feels disgusted by it. He shivers at the thought of that happening to him and cannot even make himself look at Chaos for too long. For all he knew that could be him in the years to come.

Chaos suddenly turns and crawls towards the wall, still shivering and yelling. Anthony sees the kid jerk his chin up and Chaos falls over, gasping in pain. He retches to the side and the stumbles to the glass wall.

"You call yourself *fair*?" Chaos demands, voice raspy. "*He* is the one who has done more harm than I. Why not punish *him*? Why let *him* go free?"

"A deal was struck that favored both parties," the King says. "She has no intentions of letting you go and even offered forms of torture to use on you. Quite a pleasant girl, really. I would never have thought of them."

"How is that fair?" he screams. "By what judgment have I failed to pass?"

"The fallouts of a man in power certainly do come harsher than of a man of poor status," the King agrees. "I was unaware of any of your intentions until I was judging you. I saw through your past, of your deeds. To think all those laws you placed were so no one else could overpower you. It would have been a wonderful idea, really, but you crossed a line when you wanted the humans gone."

Anthony looks at the King with surprise. The King stares coldly at Chaos, who appears just as confused.

"The humans will die out on their own," Chaos argues. "I only believe we should take their Cores, gain power and then become the dominant race. How is that wrong?"

The King sighs and twirls a scepter Anthony had not noticed before. "Humans are fickle creatures. They will fight each other, terrorize each other, and mercilessly kill each other for bountiful reasons. That is in their nature and that will always stay. But!" He looks at both Anthony and Chaos equally with the single word, stopping his rapid twirling. "But they have also been known to be kind to each other, to help and care and some will even try to save others at their life's cost. Humans are resilient and determined; something you do not appear to fully understand. They are not perfect, nor will they ever be able to be perfect, but they will always change." He sighs heavily. "I cannot allow you to destroy such an interesting race, Chaos. You are powerful enough to do it – at least, you were – but it is also a fool's journey."

Chaos knots his bloody, slowly regenerating hands into fists. "You have yet to tell me how I have failed in your judging."

"I weighed your decisions on a scale based on your position in our world. Each good action weighed slightly less than a negative action. Should they have been balanced you would be reinstated at the very beginning. Should the positive outweigh the negative you would have been placed right back in your original position. Unfortunately you got the final options. Negative actions while in higher power, using your position for selfish gain, and even threatening the life of a contracted human...all of that weighs much heavier on the scale than any good action possibly could. Not to say Anthony's decisions and actions had been any better but he had someone to bail him out – *this* time." Smiling cruelly, the King wishes Chaos a goodbye and jerks his chin again. Chaos starts to scream again but his voice is muted.

"I should be enduring the same," Anthony states to the King as they walk down another hallway.

"Oh no, yours would have been worse," the King states happily. "I would have enjoyed yours much more. Still, Alice promises me that you will be in for more punishment with her than here. I do not understand how a human could punish more than I but perhaps she can." They stop outside a door and the King opens it, letting Anthony see a small bedroom. "Get some rest, change clothes, wash up, do what you want. We will be leaving in the morning."

Pushing him in, the King locks the door behind Anthony. Sighing, Anthony falls onto a bed to rest for a little bit but his mind falls to Alice. Why save him? He gave her no reason to do such an action, had given her the reins to run away, but she refused to take it. She had saved him. How strange, to think she had saved him for once. Although, as he thinks about it, how much had she truly saved him?

Eventually, he goes into the Wash Room and sees himself in a mirror. He blinks in surprise. His eyes are blue, no longer red. Another ache in his chest reminds him of why and he proceeds to straighten himself to look more presentable than before. He drinks more water before laying to rest again. He manages scarce sleep and the King comes to retrieve him all too soon.

As they walk, Anthony is very aware of the emblem the King carries with great care. As they step outside the barrier he is greeted by harsh sunlight, cold air and a death glare from Alice. She walks up to him and slams her hand across his face – twice, for good measures. Anthony had never been aware of how much strength she has in her slaps.

Without saying anything to him, she turns towards the King. "His Core, I presume?"

He nods and hands it to her. Anthony notices how careful she is with her movements and it takes him only a moment longer to notice her arm in a sling.

"She is recovering nicely," Serene tells him, catching Anthony's eyes. "They have her arm in a sling to restrain it. Little good that has done, really, but they insist on it."

"I thank you for your cooperation," Alice says to the King. "How is Chaos handling himself?"

For the first time, Anthony hears the King laugh loudly and happily. "He hardly stops screaming! It will be a miracle if he does not go mute before the end. Honestly, Alice, you are quite a genius."

"I try my best," she replies. She turns a glare towards Anthony again. "Anthony, do you understand how late you are?"

"What?" he asks in surprise.

"When you are rescuing someone, you try to come *before* they are injured," she states. "Not only that but you are very behind on scheduling and working with the help. They are in a frenzy trying to compensate for your sudden, unexcused and unplanned absence. Good luck in trying to explain that one away. You move differently now, they will obviously notice a difference."

She continues on and both Serene and the King stare at her in shock. She lists off many different things that need to be done and then stares at Anthony with her hands on her hips when she finishes.

Anthony throws his head back and laughs. Although startled at first, relief soon overtakes him and he laughs harder. After he sits down he starts to compose himself, chuckling nonetheless. He had certainly expected something much more different than this but he should have known.

"What do you find so humorous?" Alice demands.

Gathering his composure, he says between laughs, "Nothing, Miss Alice."

"That would be *Queen* Alice to you," she snaps. "If it was nothing, then you would not be on the ground, getting your pants dirty. Honestly, has returning you into a human caused you to lose intelligence?"

"I honestly think it has, Alice," the King says. "His intelligence certainly has dropped."

"If he had any to start with," Alice replies.

Chuckling again, Anthony says, "I am simply so very glad to be back, Miss Alice."

Epilogue

Two scruffy workers stumble into Show Room and are surprised to see their Queen sitting in a wooden chair, her legs pulled into the seat and a bored look on her face while her butler, close by her chair, is smiling and trying not to laugh. Her mouth is half open as though the worker's entrance cut her off mid-sentence. Their first thought is that she looks like a doll but they had heard many rumors of the Queen before now. They are both well aware how deceiving looks can be.

"My Queen," the first worker says, kneeling. The second follows quickly behind.

"Take a seat," Alice says, gesturing towards the two other chairs and composing herself in the same motion. She places her feet on the ground and sits straight, an air of authority surrounds her. Her feet are bare, the workers notice. "Honestly, to think people would still try to kneel when they come in here! I thought moving these meetings from the Throne Room to here would have changed that."

"It is only out of respect, my Queen," the second says, taking his seat. The first glares at him, but the second only shrugs. "We are here to report on the construction work."

"How is that going?" Alice asks casually. "I heard there were problems with bandits. I hope my guards have kept you safe."

"They have done just that, my Queen," the first says. "We are over halfway finished. Do you honestly believe that these barricades will help, though? Some of the farmers are demanding to leave open areas for more fertile fields. Some of the workers are getting hesitant to work."

After a few moments of consideration, Alice asks, "Is it possible to do both?"

"Excuse me?" the second asks.

"Is it possible to leave a portion of the walls unsupported? It would need to be easily repairable and able to support the weight of any floods that the farmers do not need but still able to be taken down if the farmers require it."

"My Queen, with all due respect, that seems impossible," the first says. "We would have to start from the beginning even if it was possible."

Alice pauses for a moment, considering what they are saying. Then she looks at them oddly. "Good sirs," she says, "if it was the farmers who complained about the flooding to begin with, why are they protesting the walls now?"

"They worry for their fields," the first claims. "We are only messengers, my Queen. Not the farmers themselves."

"Why did the construction manager not come to me?" Alice asks curiously. "I doubt the manager would only send two workers on their own for such a problem. If the workers were starting to hesitate, then the manager would have sent all those hesitating to me. If the farmers were complaining, they should know to come to me as they did to request the walls." Alice looks at their faces carefully before narrowing her eyes. "I have not seen you two before. I may not know everyone in my kingdom but I certainly know all who work in this area. Tell me, what are you lying about?"

For a moment neither say a word. Then the second one stands and says, "My Queen, we are mere messengers of this situation. We have not yet told the manager in worry that more problems would arise. As for not knowing us, we have only been here a few months."

"Where was your previous home?"

Miss Alice

When the first stands up, Anthony clamps his hand on their shoulders. Both jump in surprise, wondering how he moved behind them. Only seconds ago had he been right next to the Queen!

"I would not recommend trying anything," he says. "You will not get very far. Just tell the truth and all will be fine."

"The north," the second says. "We lived under the late King's rule and only recently traveled down here. We were running short on money."

"I find it strange that I never heard news of new arrivals," Alice says. "Have you heard any news, Anthony?"

He shakes his head. "People would have been buzzing around at the news of arrivals from the late King's capital. After all, only the richest could live so close to the castle."

"What should I make of this, then?" Alice wonders. She stands up and walks closer to them. "Two new members in my quaint town who were never spoken of nor have I seen before now. Two new members who are coming directly to me to voice their concerns without first informing their manager. You are burying yourselves deeper, good sirs."

Moving quickly, Alice snatches the gun from the first worker's waist and studies it carefully. She finds a symbol on it and then laughs coldly. She drops it on the floor and then kicks it back, hearing its *clank* as it hits the wall behind her.

"I should have known that you would come from the kingdom across the river," she says. "Of course you would oppose the walls, although not for the sake of the farmers'." Alice walks across the room into a drawer, pulling out her own gun, cocking it in a lightning fast movement and points it directly at the first's head. "Beg for your life."

"I would never stoop to that," snaps the first. "Your assumptions are incorrect."

Unfortunately for the first, the second does start to beg. He admits to what Alice needs to hear and she smiles while walking towards him. Once she is directly in front of him she positions the gun directly in the center of his head and pulls the trigger.

He slumps to the ground and Alice laughs. The second worker looks at her in both fear and confusion, not a single wound on his body.

"Was the truth so hard to tell?" she asks him. "Honestly, you are quite a horrible spy and instigator. You do not tell your secrets so willingly, especially when a gun is pointed at you. Now you get to go back to your kingdom and tell your King and Queen what has happened here. You will go alive, the both of you. Tell your King of the kindness of myself and give him my best regards."

Turning her back on them she places the empty gun and her new gun inside the drawer. After locking it she proceeds to walk to the door. Before Alice has the door open she hears someone fall to the ground and she sighs.

"What hopeless creatures," Alice says. "Anthony, prepare their wagon ride home. Inform the guards to tighten their security around the construction site as well."

"Of course, Miss Alice," he says.

Snorting, Alice walks out the room and is flanked by Serene who looks surprised.

"You are here for a reason other than to discuss my reasons for not killing the spies," Alice says. "Get to that first."

Nodding, Serene twirls her red and blonde hair together as she asks for the report the Demon King requested. They go into Alice's Study and Serene retrieves the documents, placing them inside of a bag for safe keeping.

"How is Chaos?" Alice asks.

"Surviving, although I doubt that is what you should call it," Serene replies, shuddering. "You and the King are certainly a terrifying pair. He sits there and watches Chaos all the time with a sick grin on his face. It reminds me of you."

Smiling, Alice says, "I thank you for the compliment. Will the King be visiting me any time soon?"

"He wishes to," Serene says. "Although I am not when. How are you doing after your injury?"

"The doctors say my shoulder will never be completely healed. I do not expect it to be a big problem, though. Otherwise I am well. Have you found yourself a contracted yet?"

She shakes her head. "No time. I do not believe I will get free time until all of this blows over. Honestly, Anthony is forever causing trouble for me. Speaking of...Anthony!"

Anthony turns his head to Serene who is once again startled by his eyes. Quickly she shakes it off, knowing she will have to get used to it sometime.

"I can take care of that for you," she says. "If Alice will let me, of course. My apologies for eavesdropping Alice, but I am heading across the river. The King wants me to investigate a particular problem over there."

"The guards should know you well enough," Alice says. "Fine. Anthony, help Serene get them to the wagons and send her off. Bring lunch into the Meeting Room afterwards. I am going to a meeting with Sir Smith and the other generals so plan accordingly."

"I believe that Serene will be helping me load the men into their wagon rather than vice versa," Anthony replies, smiling. "I will get to it, Miss Alice."

With a shake of her head, Alice moves quickly and walks into the Meeting Room last. No one stands as she enters, choosing instead to nod respectfully towards her. She sits in her spot and Sir Smith starts his run down on the situation. Most neighboring towns and kingdoms are raising their military in case of attack from Alice's army. Alice has no plan on attacking them yet, as they have not posed a threat to her. As for the villages inside of Alice's kingdom they are thriving with the kind spring and the farmers are not predicting anything to disrupt their crops.

In the months after Anthony returned, Alice rarely had a moment to spare. Having first to restore order inside her manor, Alice then focused on her kingdom. She started with the announcement of the King's death which sent the kingdom into a frenzy. Alice's coronation came immediately after his funeral and the number of guards around their new Queen greatly increased. Many were initially wary of a single, young female ruler but most eventually banished their worries. Although she is not the perfect ruler and has already made many mistakes, she quickly fixes them and carries on.

Many of the late King's allies have become strong allies to the young Queen while her own personal alliances grew stronger. Just as her allies grew, her enemies immediately multiplied drastically. Those who had strained relationships quickly came to trust or hate her for one reason or another. The neutral village in the southeast had quickly joined peace treaties with Alice once she was declared Queen, while Lord Raymond's country had defied her almost immediately, none to her surprise.

For Anthony adjusting to his new life is harder than he initially thought. With new limits and restraints, the help had to work harder until Anthony learned his new pace. Once he adjusted on that front, he became curious to the emblem that held his Core. Alice, knowing more than all but the King himself, took to explaining the emblem to him. His Core was trapped within metallic Fate Weavers, a creation of the Demon King specifically for this. She could administer pain to him depending on the situation just as the King could. Only they could touch the emblem as a way to prevent accidental problems. Anthony was more so confused by his ability to have a Core which Serene took care of explaining. Once you become a Demon you lose a large portion of your Core as you have died but they retain a small portion. As such the King removed the Core from Anthony but managed to keep it slightly attached. Serene is unsure how the King managed such a trick. When Anthony asked the King all he would say was, "King's secret."

When Anthony had received the chance he apologized to Alice for breaking his long-forgotten promise and for not rescuing her before she received her injuries. He had never seen Alice at a loss for words before and he laughed at it. Alice had recovered from her stupor enough to mumble her thanks and walk off. Anthony could have sworn he saw her blushing but he could not say for sure.

As he thought Alice had not stopped going to town to get the simple pastries at least once a month. To his surprise she did not move to the late King's castle. Many of the kingdom's people were surprised to have their Queen so close to borders and not within their protection but Alice simply waved them off. He cannot understand the silly girl and he wishes that he could just give up trying, but his curiosity has reached a new high. She acts as though nothing has changed for her, but Anthony notices small differences. She walks differently, even behaves slightly different. Less childish or maybe more mature. Either way the changes are very small and only those within the manor have truly noticed such changes.

Serene takes every opportunity to tease Anthony about new position as a "human slave." She also takes it upon herself to drill him on information about Alice, and to yell at him again for leaving her in charge of the young Queen without being first informed. Anthony had smiled at her yells, not replying to her frustration. He has also stopped giving so much information about Alice, as Serene does not understand most of his answers.

The Demon King has certainly had his own fun. He does watch Chaos with interest every day for long stretches of the day but he has decided to visit Alice whenever he can. He asks for her reports on what Anthony has done during the times he cannot reach her and has already visited her a few times. Alice is not sure what he does to make him so busy but she never questions him.

Every now and again tiny rumors will spread of Alice spending much time with a strange boy and Alice lets the rumors go around as they please. No one in the kingdom knows who the boy is and most of the help does not even think twice about Alice being with a strange individual anymore. They have become quite used to the oddness that circles the young Queen.

While Alice concludes her meeting with Sir Smith, Anthony walks into the room offering drinks to the room's occupants. Most request water or tea, while others ask if they could have some form of alcohol, which Sir Smith immediately denies. When Anthony places Alice's glass in front of her she gives him thanks for the whole room and Anthony smiles at her.

"I work to please," he says, a joking grin on his lips.

Snorting, Alice wraps up the meeting just as Serene pops her head in.

"My Queen," she says, taking notice of the others in the room. "You have a guest."

Before Alice can think twice, the Demon King barrels into the room and hugs Alice.

"I am sorry for making you write a report when I did manage to get free time," he says. "I did not know I would be receiving time to visit until Serene came in. What were you discussing in here, Alice?"

Many of the room's occupants gawk at the boy and then stare at Alice as they waiting for her to yell at him but she simply smiles and introduces the King to Sir Smith. After introductions Sir Smith tells him some of what they had been discussing.

"What shall I address you as?" Sir Smith asks.

"Just the King," the boy says. "Alice thinks quite highly of you. I hope you do not disappoint her." He nods, his eyes change to mirror Alice's, move to mimic Sir Smith's and then speed along to different colors. Afterwards his eyes widen in understanding. "Ah, so you are the brilliant teacher who made Alice so wonderful! Glorious! It is quite an honor to meet you, then!"

Alice chuckles under her breath and Anthony looks on in mild curiosity.

"I cannot take that much credit," Sir Smith manages, surprised by the boy. "She is a wonderful student. A natural born ruler. I only helped her refine the skills she had."

Miss Alice

"I do not believe that is true," the King says, smiling. "It was wonderful to meet you, Sir Smith. I would like to borrow your Queen for a little while, though. Alice?"

Nodding, Alice dismisses the meeting once again and, once everyone but Alice's small group has cleared out, the King's smile drops to a serious frown. He studies Anthony carefully.

"I have only read the reports on what Alice has said," he states, a threat dripping from his voice, "and I highly disbelieve Alice would lie to me or to anyone. But I would like to get one thing straight. You are getting this second chance because someone has decided your life is worth it and, because of that, everything good you do is now worth slightly less than before and your bad is heavier. When you are judged you better have collected enough good to put Alice through all this."

Anthony nods his head. "I understand," he says. "Of course, what if Alice decides to keep me as her slave forever, even after she has become a Demon? What will you do then?"

"I highly doubt that will happen," Alice replies with a snort.

"People only get second chances once," the King replies flatly. "You do not receive a second chance for a second chance."

Again Anthony nods his head and then the King is all smiles again.

"What are you planning for the rest of the day?" he asks excitedly to Alice.

"Well I have some things to attend to later in the day," Alice says, "but I believe now would be a fair time to go to town. Anthony, would you please inform Sir Smith that I will be going out for a bit? He will inform everyone else in the manor. You know how they worry."

He nods and goes off, Serene following after a moment.

"Does she normally trail him like a lost puppy?" the King asks.

"Not always," Alice replies. "It certainly has become more common, though."

Snickering, the King says, "I bet she *likes* him."

"That would certainly be the day," Alice remarks. "I could never imagine those two being in the same room for long." Alice gives a small smile. "Let us go outside. They can meet us there."

Once the King nods excitedly, Alice and the King walk outside. The King runs around in the front yard of the manor and Alice sits on the steps and watches in complete amusement as the boy runs around. She wonders if he has had the chance to do this before or if he remembers such a time when he could. Either way it is hard to believe this rambunctious little boy is the King of Demons.

Back inside the house Anthony and Serene have successfully informed Sir Smith of their departure and he has promised to inform the others should they ask. As they are walking back, Serene stops Anthony.

"We need to hurry back," Anthony says. "Alice will not be happy if we do not get back as quickly as possible."

"I just need to ask you two things," she says, completely serious. "First off, what game are you playing?"

"The game that keeps me living for a little bit longer?" Anthony says questioningly.

"With Alice and the King," she says exasperated. "I really think you lost some intelligence when you became a human, Anthony."

"As far as I know I am not playing any game," he says with a smile. "I stopped planning when I decided to ask you for help. Things seem to be much more enjoyable that way. Do you think humans normally act like that? If so I am starting to understand how they can be so relaxed. It is quite a wonderful feeling, Serene, to not have to worry about everything years in advance."

Serene sighs. "If you will not tell me: fine. The other thing I wanted to know: Alice."

"Serene, I have told you already that I refuse to answer any more questions about Alice."

"This one is only partially directed towards Alice." The two stare at each other for a long time before Anthony sighs and waves his hand. Serene smiles gloatingly. "Am I the only one to notice the change in Alice's behavior?"

"How so?"

"She seems...happier whenever we all go into town."

Anthony chuckles softly. "Alice has never been much of a person to have friends, as you can well imagine. I believe the King is the closest she has ever had to someone her own age being near her for a long period of time, even if he is technically much older. You see how he acts around her and Alice takes comfort in it. Who knows? Maybe being best friends with the Demon King will be good for her."

"I highly doubt it will be good for anyone else," Serene states. "Most everyone feared her because of you but now she has a nonthreatening-looking boy that could torture them for all eternity." Serene shivers. "I almost fear her with the power she has at her disposal."

Chuckling, Anthony shakes his head at Serene. "Most everyone fears Alice because she is intelligent and able to think ahead of her opponent. You should see her when she plays chess with visiting Lords. How easily she can manipulate them!"

"If you say so."

"Besides, Alice would never allow the King nor me to hurt anyone within her kingdom unless they act upon her life first."

Jerking her head in surprise, she looks towards his serious face. "What makes you think that?"

Smiling, Anthony does not answer. Just beckons her to follow him. Once they make it outside they find the King sprawled out on the grass and Alice chiding him about getting his clothes dirty.

"Miss Alice!" Anthony calls and Alice turns her head towards his voice. "Are you ready to go?"

Nodding, she helps the King up and pops him on the head for getting so dirty, sending him into a fit of laughter. He pulls her towards the end of the yard and Anthony notices she does not have shoes on.

"Miss Alice!" Anthony yells. "Why are you not wearing shoes?"

"You never got them for me," Alice replies, pulling the King to a stop.

"You never requested them," Anthony reminds her.

"When have I ever willingly worn shoes, Anthony?"

He sighs and then turns to Serene. "Would you please go get her some shoes?"

"Of course," she says sarcastically. "Would you like me to fetch you a hat and coat as well?"

"You are the fastest between us and will easily catch up," Anthony reminds her. "Besides, you are not the one who has their life on the line."

"But, Anthony, this is such a good deed for you to do!"

For a long minute they stare at each other before Serene finally breaks it and rushes back inside.

Anthony starts to move towards them when he sees the King give a mischievous smile. Pausing, Anthony remembers back to when he misplaced Alice, the boy who stopped him before he left. Anthony looks at the King and the King looks back at him with his impish grin.

"Are you coming, Mister Anthony?" the King calls out, ignoring Alice's look. Shaking his head, he turns to Alice. "Geez, Alice. What do you see in him?"

Miss Alice

They wait impatiently for Anthony to start walking again and then the King grabs Alice's hand and drags her off, leaving Anthony to sprint to catch up to the kids. Alice shouts for the King to slow down but the King ignores her. By the time Anthony does reach them, he collapses on the ground from exhaustion. Alice immediately starts to scold him and Anthony apologizes, standing after a few seconds and dusting himself off.

"Where did Serene run off to?" the King asks, noticing the missing Demon.

"She went to get Alice's shoes for me," Anthony replies, still panting. Anthony catches the King's sharp look and simply shrugs. "She can get here much faster than I and will be able to catch up much easier than I could."

"Fair enough," Alice says. "We should wait for Serene. It is not a long walk, but I do not think I can go on without something on my feet."

"Anthony could always carry you," the King states.

"It is always an option," Anthony agrees with a smile.

Alice shakes her head. "Serene should be here soon, correct? We will wait."

The King sits down with a sigh and Anthony chuckles at him. While they wait, Anthony keeps sending the boy looks, disbelieving that he is the same boy that was inside Alice's manor. The King pretends not to see Anthony but his puckish smile suggests his knowledge. Once Serene arrives and once Alice has her shoes on properly, they continue on.

As soon as they get into town, the King quickly changes from mischievous to childish in a blink of the eye. He wants to go into every shop, try every treat, buy one of everything. People wave to their Queen and make openings for her to get through and most offer smiles to her. Alice kindly returns their waves and smiles, thank them for giving her space to move in crowded areas and the people simply melt over it. The King snickers at their reactions and whispers to a smiling Anthony, the two sharing a twisted joke on the beloved human Queen.

Eventually they all get hungry and they decide upon a quaint eatery that Alice is quite fond of. They all make small chatter as they wait for their food. After some time Alice stands to excuse herself momentarily and she bumps into someone. She loses her balance and falls back into her chair.

"My apologies, sir," Alice says professionally. "I did not see you there."

"Watch where you're going next time," the man snaps. "Don't think you're so special because you sit on top of a throne."

"She apologized," Anthony says darkly. "Sit back down, sir, and do not instigate a scene."

"Oh shut up," the man snaps. "I doubt any of you have had to work a day in your lives. You just sit inside a comfy house and order everyone else around."

"Sir, I recommend you leaving this eatery," the King says, voice flat. "If you know what is good for you, that is."

"You're just a kid. Don't try to talk so big."

A chill blankets the room as the King stands up. Perhaps it is Alice's imagination, but the shadows seem to shrink back as he stands. The King looks up at the man with a cold stare and the man starts to back up.

"In three seconds," he says, "you will be in unbearable agony. You can get out of here in those three seconds or you can stay. Your choice."

For a moment, the man looks ready to run but, before he can take a step, he falls to the ground, gasping for air he cannot seem to pull in correctly. His mouth opens and closes like a fish out of water and the King crouches beside the man, tilting his head in curiosity.

"Do you understand what happens when you freeze time around one person?" he asks the man. "It causes everything to still, meaning no oxygen can come to you. Of course, I would never let you simply pass out on me. I will make sure your lungs explode and keep you alive even afterwards."

"Enough!"

Jerking up and spinning around, the King is met with a brisk slap and he falls to the ground. As soon as he does the spell is broken and the man pulls in air before leaving in a hurry.

"What were you thinking?" Alice demands.

"He was being rude to his ruler," the King replies. "He needed to learn his place."

"There will always be people who oppose their rulers," Alice snaps. "No matter how liked the ruler is, there will always be people who see them as bad. That is how a kingdom works. Without opposition, there will not be support. Without support, you cannot have a kingdom." Leaning close to the King, she whispers, "These people are mine to judge and punish as I see fit. As long as they are alive you are not the judge, do you understand me?"

Unable to form words the King just nods. Accepting that, Alice looks around the eatery and notices that no one seems to be looking at them, some embarrassed but others looking guilty.

"To them, nothing happened," the King says. "They are only aware of the man being rude to you and then him running. Time was at a brief standstill. You are welcome."

After that the group eats their food without much talk. Once they are out the King takes only a few minutes before he is bouncing around at every new sight.

As the sun starts to set and the King becomes weary they drop by the bakery. Once inside Alice feels a sense of warmth and she licks her lips in expectation of her treat. The owner welcomes them heartily and makes a brief conversation with Alice before handing her a box of her cream puffs. Of course the King quickly makes his own order and Alice leads them all out after thanking and paying the owner for the treats.

Serene, Anthony, and the King all watch Alice curiously as she herself acts very childishly for a little bit. She makes a mess as she devours the tiny pastries and licks her fingers. The King teases her about her manners and she blushes slightly but does not break her swift devour of the treats.

When the King steals and eats one, he makes a face and stares at Alice oddly.

"These are so *boring*," he complains. "How can you eat these things?"

"Cream puffs are quite delicious!" Alice replies indignantly.

"Miss Alice, I must admit that they are quite a plain pastry," Anthony tells her. "They are also the only dessert that you insist on making a mess all over your face when eating."

They walk on for a little bit in silence as Alice ponders on her response. She eats two more and then frowns at the little left over in her box. Before any of them notice they are coming upon Alice's manor and all know that Alice will be going back to work as soon as she goes back inside. So they stop just at the edge of her yard and Alice looks at them all.

"A cream puff is simple," she finally says. "No matter what the day or year, the cream puff will always be the same thing. Compared to all the others, this small thing is far too plain. A little simplicity every now and again is quite good for the mind, would you not agree?" Alice yawns and then gives Serene and the King a business-like smile. "It was nice to see you both again. Be safe on your return. I will be awaiting your next visit."

Serene nods but stays quiet.

"I hope you live a long and successful life, Queen Alice," the King says. "The next time we meet might be in a day or years away. I am expecting great things from you." He turns a sharp glare towards

Anthony. "Keep her safe. Should her death be untimely you will be the first I drag down."

"She will be protected to my fullest extent," Anthony says. "I can swear upon that."

Nodding, the King turns away and waves without looking back. He and Serene slip back into the King's barrier quickly once the King became enveloped in shadows.

"That sounded like a final goodbye," Serene states once inside the King's mansion.

"Perhaps it was," the King says. "I surely do not know. That silly human Queen, though.... She intrigues me. Remind me to send her a gift one of these days, will you?"

"Of course," Serene says. "Why not send it to her now?"

"If you could see as I do, Serene the Harpy, you would understand," the King says with a sigh. He turns away and brings out a white feather and frowns deeply. "I hope you know that I expect you to watch them from afar for now."

"I figured as much."

"Good. You are dismissed." He steps into the shadows of the room and disappears.

After he disappears Serene quickly walks back to her room where she quickly falls asleep. She dreams of the complicated human that enjoys such a simple pastry and wonders what the child will do with her life ahead of her.

At Alice's manor, as the night fully settles in, Anthony shakes Alice partially awake.

Anthony sighs but smiles at her. "Still overworking yourself, Miss Alice?" he asks quietly. He manages to put Alice on his back and carries her to her room, tucking her into her bed carefully. He sets out her dress for tomorrow and takes down the list from the morning of things to do before putting up another.

Just as he is leaving, Alice mumbles, "Thank you for bringing me to bed."

"Of course, Miss Alice." He stuffs the paper inside his pocket. "Friends do help each other from time to time."

"You are not my friend," she grumbles.

"Am I at least your servant?"

"We can settle on allies, I guess."

"If that is what you wish, Miss Alice."

"That would be Queen Alice."

"Silly me. How could I forget? Anything else Miss Alice?"

She says something that Anthony does not catch. She is asleep before Anthony can ask her for a restate. Shaking his head he walks out and bumps into an eavesdropping maid, who falls back in embarrassment.

"I-I'm so sorry, Mister Anthony!" she says.

"No worries," he says kindly and then offers a hand to help her up.

Taking his hand, they remain in silence. Anthony can tell the maid wants to ask him something so he waits with a smile on his face.

Finally, the maid asks, "You're Queen Alice's friend, then? The young Queen finally has herself a friend?"

Chuckling softly, he helps the maid gather herself. "More like an allied manservant. Alice never has friends."

"Honestly, that girl is so stubborn." The maid sighs but smiles at him. "At least she can depend on someone now."

"It is certainly a start," Anthony agrees. He looks at Alice's door and smiles. "Perhaps the most glorious start so far."

Thank You

Thanks to all that read this: every single person who reads it lifts my spirits a bit more and tells me I'm doing something right.

Thanks to my Mom for everything she's done and allowing my imagination to run wild (no matter how weird it may have been). Also for putting up with me when I kept spoiling everything. Bigger thanks for dealing with me during our editing session.

Thank you Dan for actually getting the initial writing process going. If you hadn't asked to see my writing initially, Miss Alice would never have gotten here. You deserve a lot of thanks for that alone.

Thanks Sarah S for helping me along the way and kicking my butt when I didn't work on Miss Alice. Also thanks for dealing with my rants and random ideas that didn't make it. You practically MADE me write this story a few times.

Thank you Julia for making Anthony a pervert-prostitute. Seriously, I could have lived without those thoughts but the laughs made it worthwhile.

Thanks to my brother for catching my mistakes the first few copies made. Your pairing certainly is a different take on things but it won't happen. Sorry!

Thanks to my sister and brother (in law). When we watched videos late at night it would help a lot to relieve stress and Brian your antics were always super funny. You guys were a great way to spend time away from writing. Also, Chelsie, thanks for rationalizing the thousands of edits I had to go through (even if you thought I wasn't appreciative, I really am).

Sarah Gastright

Thanks Aurora for all the pictures! The cover is awesome and exactly as I envisioned it. It can't be easy to deal with my vague instructions or to deal with me in general in picture-taking situations.

Big thanks to Eddie Hughes and Deep Sea Publishing for seeing the glitter that I couldn't. You picked Miss Alice up and made it something I could never imagine.

Thanks to those who kept me going because, honestly, we wouldn't be here otherwise, would we?

Sneak Peak of Book Two:

She stands in front of a mirror, examining her dress. A white dress, as the ceremony requires, with long fitted sleeves and a fitted top, both of soft silk. Her skirt poofs at her waist in the same material, just long enough to cover her feet from view. Although a rather plain dress, it suits her needs just fine.

When the door opens, she hardly has to look away from the mirror to know who it is.

"Are you ready?" asks the other Queen.

"Of course," she replies. Picking up a comb she runs it once again through her pale blonde hair. Another look in the mirror and she places a smile on her face. *Focus,* she orders herself. *You are happy.*

"Then we should hurry," replies the other Queen. "We must not keep the ceremony from starting."

Looking at the other Queen's hand, the young girl reaches out and hesitates before grasping it firmly. They walk through doors and down a long church aisle. As the cheery bells ring, light falls against the bride's face, exposing her clouded gray eyes.

Once deposited at her spot, the other Queen moves behind the groom who makes the pale bride seem dark in comparison.

"We are here today," begins the Priest a bit hesitantly, "to unite these two in holy matrimony."

As the ceremony progresses, people come in and look on in surprise. They had not been informed of a royal wedding! Why would their Queen hide it from them? They take their seat and watch as their beloved Queen marries some stranger.

"Do you promise to love this woman in sickness and in health, through good times and bad times?" asks the Priest to the groom.

He feels the other Queen grinning behind him. "I do," he says, staring at his bride with a smile.

While the priest repeats the same question to the bride, she tries not to hear the murmurs of those in her village or show how hard she grips the groom's hands. *If only they knew,* she thinks.

"...and bad times?"

"I—" She pauses as she feels a sudden chill through the church, sees the shadows receding. Everything in the bright church takes on a gray hue and, no matter how hard she tries to form the syllables of "do" she cannot make them appear.

Doors burst open and her stomach sinks.

"Alice!" yells the Demon King. Followed by a much more familiar voice.

Behind her, someone covers her mouth with a hand and presses something metallic to her head.

"Hello Miss Alice," her butler, Anthony, whispers.

All the shadows appear correctly, the gray disappearing. Both the groom and other Queen jerk back in surprise. Anthony tugs her to face the startled crowd and then jerks her back. Alice tries to speak but Anthony's hand – which is always gloved – muffles all her words. Alice spies the Demon King hurrying towards the other Queen and she closes her eyes.

No, no, no, she thinks fearfully. *This is not supposed to happen. Why are they here? They should be elsewhere!*

"If anyone tries to speak or move," Anthony calls out, sounding more conversational than he should, "the Queen's head will not look this pretty."

Everyone in the church freezes, afraid to even breathe. Unaffected by Anthony's warning, the Demon King walks up to the other Queen and presses his hand to her stomach before doing the same to the startled groom. She and he freeze in their spots and then the Demon King walks over to Alice, his eyes flashing red and black.

"I will never allow you to belong to them," he snarls, so low Alice almost misses it. "Next time you decide to solve a problem like this on your own, *Alice*, you better think twice and come to me." He turns around from them and addresses the terrified mass. "The wedding is over. Go home." Turning back around to look at Anthony, he whispers, "Take her somewhere safe. Do not let anyone get near her until I and Serene are there, understand me?"

"Yes, your Majesty," Anthony replies with a smile. "Well, Miss Alice, shall we be going?"

About the Author

When she was younger, Sarah Gastright was always writing. Whether it was scribbles on construction paper, or poems in her journal, she was always putting words on paper. Then, as she got older, she started writing stories that slowly turned into full-length novels, and that's when *Miss Alice* was born. At the age of 15, she sat down at her laptop in the early hours of New Years day 2013 and started the yearlong journey of her breakout novel.

Sarah Gastright lives in Columbia, South Carolina. Although writing is her passion, she enjoys playing video games, watching Roosterteeth on YouTube, and hanging out with her dog, Schnoodle.

Upcoming Books and Information

Deep Sea Publishing (DSP) is pleased to provide you this great book by Sarah Gastright. If you like this story, you'll also enjoy:

Let Sleeping Dragons Lie, by Tryone Burson (DSP Winner)

The Gallivan Legacy, by Sable Lewis (DSP Winner)

Hardt's Tale, by Gwendolyn Druyor (DSP Winner)

The Good Fight, by Ophelia Hu (DSP Winner)

The Bryant Family Chronicles, by Eddie Hughes (Readers Choice Winner)

These award-winning works are available in paperback and eBook form at Deep Sea Publishing's Online Store, Amazon, Apple's iBookstore, and BarnesandNoble.com. The DSP website also lists the shops and bookstores that carry the books. These books can be ordered from any bookstore as well.

Deep Sea Publishing (DSP) is a Florida-based company that sells novels, young adult/teen fiction, children's books, photography books, and reference guides. The website mentioned below supplies details on all DSP publications and the expected release dates of new material.

www.deepseapublishing.com

www.ingramcontent.com/pod-product-compliance
Lightning Source LLC
Chambersburg PA
CBHW060812120626
46557CB00001B/191